MW01138894

Relentless

Book One of the Shattered Hearts Series

CASSIA LEO

Relentless

For Chris.

None of this would be possible without you.

Note to Reader

Music is an important part of this series. Some chapters in this book begin with a musical note. The musical note indicates there is a song on the *Relentless* playlist that pertains to or is mentioned in that chapter. Please feel free to open the playlist on a computer or mobile device and listen as you read.

The playlist is available on YouTube at:
http://bit.ly/relentlessplaylist

The playlist is available on Spotify at:
http://bit.ly/relentlessplaylists

CHAPTER ONE

Relentless Addiction

MOM IS TOO *tired to play hide-and-seek. Her stomach hurts so she took some medicine to make it feel better. I don't like it when she's sick. Grandma Patty doesn't know about Mom's stomachaches and I haven't seen Grandma in a few weeks, but I'm starting to think I should tell her.*

Mom is asleep on the sofa; at least, I think she's asleep. I can't really tell the difference anymore. Sometimes, when I think she's sleeping, I'll try to sneak some cookies out of the cupboard. She usually hears me and yells at me to get out of the kitchen. Sometimes, she sleeps with her eyes half-open so I wave my hands in front of her eyes and make silly faces at her. She never wakes up and I always get bored after a couple of minutes. It's no fun teasing someone unless there's someone else around to laugh, and it's just Mom and me here.

Her skinny arm is stretched out over the edge of the sofa cushion and I stare at the bandage. It's too small to cover that big sore. One of those things she calls an abscess *opened last night while she was making me a grilled- cheese sandwich. Some thick, brown stuff oozed out of her arm. It reminded me of the glaze on maple donuts, but it didn't smell anything like a maple donut. The whole kitchen smelled like stinky feet when she put her arm under the water in the sink. Then she wrapped a billion paper towels around her arm and I had to eat a burnt sandwich.*

She didn't want to go to the doctor. She said that if she goes to the emergency room and shows them her arm the doctors might make her stay in the hospital for a long time. Then I'll have to live with people I don't know, people who might hurt me, until she gets better. My mom loves me a lot. She doesn't want anybody to hurt me the way she was hurt when she was nine.

Mom teaches me a lot. She isn't just my mom; she's my teacher. When she isn't sick, she teaches me math and spelling, but my favorite subject is science. I love learning about the planets the most. I want to be an astronomer when I grow up. Mom said that I can be anything I want to be if I just keep reading and learning. So that's what I do when she's sick. I read.

She's been asleep for a long time today. I've already read two chapters in my science book. Maybe I should try to wake her up. I'm hungry. I can make myself some cereal—I am *seven—but Mom promised she'd make me spaghetti today.*

I slide off the recliner and land on the mashed beige carpet that Mom always says is too dirty for me to sit on. I take two steps until I'm standing just a few inches away from her face. Her skin looks weird, sort of grayish-blue.

"Mom?" I whisper. "I'm hungry."

Something smells like a toilet and I wonder if it's the stinky abscess on her arm. I shake her shoulder a little and her head falls sideways. A glob of thick, white liquid spills from the corner of her mouth.

The memory dissolves as someone calls my name.

"Claire?"

The cash register comes into focus as the rich aroma of espresso replaces the acrid stench in my memory. I've done it again. For the third time this week, I've spaced out while taking someone's order. The last two customers were understanding, but this guy in his *Tap Out* T-shirt and veins bulging out of his smooth bald head looks like he's ready to jump over the counter and either strangle me or get his own coffee.

"Sorry, about that. What was your order?"

"Wake the fuck up, blondie. I asked for an Americano with two Splendas. Jesus fucking Christ. There are people with serious jobs who need to get to work."

I take a deep breath, my fingers trembling, as I punch the order in on the touchscreen. "Will that be all?"

Baldy rolls his eyes at me. "And the scone. Come on, come on. I gotta get the fuck out of here."

"Hey, take it easy. She's just trying to take your order," says a voice. I don't look up, but I can hear it came from the back of the line of customers.

"I already gave her my order three fucking times," Baldy barks over his shoulder. "Mind your own fucking business."

Linda comes up from behind me, placing a comforting hand on my shoulder as she sets the guy's Americano on the counter next to the bag holding his multigrain scone. She doesn't say anything, but the nasty look she casts in his direction could make an ultimate fighting champion piss his pants. Linda is the best boss in the world and one of the many reasons I still work at Beachcombers Café. All the other reasons I still work at one of the tiniest cafés in Wrightsville Beach have to do mostly with my desire to disappear after dropping out of UNC Chapel Hill ten months ago. But that's a whole other story.

Baldy peels the lid off his coffee, rolling his eyes as he peers into the cup. "I said I wanted room for cream. Are you all fucking retarded?"

Before I could reach for the cup, a guy in a suit steps out of line, grabs the cup off the counter, and dumps the entire contents into Baldy's scone bag. A loud collective gasp echoes through the café.

"Now you've got plenty of room for cream," the guy says.

I clap my hand over my mouth to stifle a laugh as Linda scrambles to get some paper towels.

The rage in Baldy's eyes is terrifying. "You motherfucker!" he roars as my white knight grins.

And what a sexy white knight he is. Even in his pressed shirt and slacks, he can't be more than twenty-two. He has an easygoing vibe about him, as if he'd rather be surfing than wearing a suit at seven in the morning. With his sun-kissed brown hair and the devious gleam in his green eyes, he reminds me of Leonardo DiCaprio in one of my favorite movies, *Titanic*.

Baldy charges my Jack Dawson, but Jack swiftly steps aside at the last moment. Baldy trips spectacularly over a waist-high display of mugs and coffee beans. All six people in the café are now standing silent as Baldy spits curses at the cracked mugs and spilled beans underneath him.

I look at my white knight and he's smiling at me, a sneaky half-smile, and I know what he's about to do.

Before Baldy can get to his feet, Jack drops a few hundred-dollar bills on the counter. "For the damages."

He winks at me as he steps on Baldy's back then hurries toward the exit with no coffee, just a huge grin that makes everybody laugh and cheer. He gives us a quick bow, showing his appreciation to the crowd, and slips through the door as Baldy lumbers to his feet.

My gaze follows Jack as he slides into his truck, one of the newer models that looks like something conceived in the wet dreams of a roughneck and a Star Wars geek. He pulls out of the parking lot and disappears down Lumina Avenue.

I have a strong urge to whisper, "I'll never let go,

Jack," but I'm pretty good at keeping my urges to mutter lines from *Titanic* to myself; especially when there's a six-foot-two 'roided-out freak staring me down. Something snaps inside me as I remember what started this whole fiasco.

I step aside so Linda can take over and I skitter away through the swinging door into the stockroom. I unfold a metal chair and sit down next to a small desk where Linda does the scheduling. Pulling my legs up, I sit cross-legged on the chair, place my hands on my knees, and close my eyes. I take a long, deep breath, focusing on nothing but the oxygen as it enters my lungs. I let the breath out slowly. A few more deep breaths and the whole incident in the café never happened.

Some people are addicted to heroin. Others are addicted to coffee. I'm addicted to meditation. No, not medication. Meditation.

Meditation doesn't just relax me; it helps me forget. It's like a friend you can count on to say just the right thing at the right time when that thing you want them to say is nothing. Meditation is the friend who intervenes when you're about to say or do something very stupid. Like three months ago, when meditation saved me from taking my own life after I realized I had become my mother.

Chapter Two

Relentless Memories

I HAVEN'T BEEN to a party with my best friend Yesenia Navarro in ten months. The last time was the Halloween bash at Joey Nassau's house where I got stuck talking to Joey's thirty-something cousin who spent three hours attempting to convince me to go back to school. I want to go to tonight's party at Annabelle Mezza's house about as much as I want to eat a spoonful of cinnamon. Tonight's party will be packed with all the people I have been successfully avoiding for ten months.

"I'll be velcroed to your side the whole night," Senia assures me as I gather my purse and a bottle of water from the kitchen counter.

Senia thinks I'm a freak because I never leave the apartment without at least one bottle of water. I've spent enough time avoiding the various other substances my mother abused. She could hardly call an addiction to water and meditating a bad thing. This doesn't stop her from trying. And true to best-friend form, every day when she comes home from work she still brings me a six-pack of my drug of choice. To say that I love living with my best friend would be a huge understatement.

"Whatever," I mutter. "It's just down the street. I'll walk home if things get too uncomfortable."

"Speaking of uncomfortable." Senia cocks an eyebrow as she examines my outfit: faded skinny jeans, a plain white tank top, a green hoodie that's three sizes too big, and a five-year-old pair of black Converse. "Is that what you're wearing?"

Senia could be a supermodel with her perfectly tanned skin, dark tousled hair, and spot-on fashion sense. At five-ten, she towers over my five-foot-six frame in her four-inch heels. She has the perfect button nose and full lips that I've always dreamed of having. My blonde hair is too thin, my nose is too small, and my upper lip is too big. Senia says it gives me a sexy pout, but she only says that to make me feel better. I'm average and I've learned to not only accept it, I embrace it.

"Don't make me say it," I reply as I unscrew the cap on the bottle of water and take a swig.

She holds up her hand to stop me. "Please don't. And, by the way, that has to be the *worst* motto ever adopted by any person ever in the history of all mankind."

I pull my keys out of my purse to lock the front door as we make our way out of the apartment. "You might be exaggerating just a little bit."

Her heels click against the pavement and I inhale a huge breath of briny ocean breeze as we walk to the covered parking spot where Senia keeps her new black Ford Focus. She isn't rolling in cash, but her parents make pretty good money with the real-estate company where their entire family works. She works in one of their satellite offices in Wilmington while the rest of the family works at the main office in Raleigh. Her parents pay her half of the rent on our apartment, her entire UNC tuition, and she gets a new car every two years on her birthday. Nothing fancy, but new.

"I get it," Senia says as she deactivates her car alarm and we slide into our seats. "You don't want to be a shallow, vacuous piece of shit like Joanie Tipton. But that doesn't mean that you have to dress for a party like you're going to work on a fucking construction site."

"Hey, I resent that. I left my tool belt at home this time," I tease her and she rolls her eyes as she turns on the stereo to her favorite EDM station.

An Ellie Goulding dance mix blasts through the speakers and Senia immediately begins bobbing her head as she pulls the car out of the parking space. She maneuvers her car around the moving truck that's half-blocking the exit out of the complex. Cora, our eighty-six-year-old landlord, must have finally found a tenant for the upstairs apartment.

"Claire!" Senia shouts as she pulls onto Lumina. "You need to renew your driver's license!"

"Senia! I live four hundred feet from where I work and I don't have a car. I don't need a driver's license just so I can be your designated driver."

I sold my car when I moved to Wrightsville Beach two and a half months ago to pay for the first and last month's rent on my apartment. Senia moved in three weeks later, once the semester ended. She claimed she did it so we could spend the summer together on the hottest surf beach on the East Coast, but I know it's so she can help me with the rent for a few months. The summer is halfway over now and she'll be moving back in with her parents in a month to go back to UNC. If I don't find another roommate or convince Linda to give me more hours at the café, I may be homeless in six months—for the third time in my life.

As soon as Senia pulls up in front of Annabelle's parents' beach house, I smell the beer and hear the laughter. My chest tightens. I focus my eyes on the water bottle in my hand, forcing myself to think of nothing else as I breathe deeply and slowly. Senia is quiet as she waits for me. She's used to my coping mechanisms.

The edges of my vision blur and everything but the bottle disappears. I think about how water is the essential element for life to flourish. I think of how it soothes and carries us, cleanses and quenches us. I imagine the water washing away every worry, every doubt about tonight and carrying it away to a clear, tranquil sea. I close my eyes and take one final deep breath as my muscles go slack and I'm completely relaxed.

I nod once and reach for the door handle. "Okay. Let's do this."

"I don't know how you do that, but it's kind of creepy and inspiring all at once."

Senia and I stroll up the walkway arm-in-arm past the lush summer garden toward the blue, two-story clapboard beach house. I spot a group of five guys standing on the porch with red Solo cups and cigarettes clutched in their hands. From his profile, I recognize the short Indian guy leaning against the porch railing. He was in the sophomore Comp Lit class I dropped out of last October. I turn my head slightly as Senia and I climb the steps to the front door, hoping none of them will recognize me.

Senia pulls open the squeaky screen door and I choke on the sweet smell of alcohol and perfume. We step further inside and the first thing I see is a gathering of a dozen or so people huddled around the sofa where a guy with a guitar is playing and singing a Jason Mraz song.

This memory is too strong to fight.

I walk through the tall door into my ninth and final foster home. As luck would have it, the woman I called Grandma Patty eight years ago was actually just our closest neighbor. I had no family to take me in after my mother died. I'm only fifteen, but I'm already more jaded and cynical than my forty-something caseworker. She flat out told me that this would be my last placement. If I screw this one up, I'll be sent to a halfway house until I turn sixteen in four months. The moment I step into the living room, I know I'll be seeing the inside of that halfway house soon.

Three guys sit around a coffee table, two of them on the sofa and one cross-legged on the floor with a guitar in his lap. The one with the guitar wears a gray beanie and his dark hair falls around his face in jagged wisps. He's humming a tune I recognize as a Beatles song my mom used to play whenever she cleaned the house: "I Want You."

The thud of my backpack hitting the floor gets his attention and he looks straight into my eyes. "Are you Claire?" he asks. His voice is smooth with just a touch of a rasp.

I nod and he immediately sets his guitar down on the floor in front of him. My body tenses as he walks toward me—as my "training" kicks in. The reason I've been in and out of foster homes for the past eight years since my mom OD'd is because of everything she taught me.

From as far back as I can remember, my mother taught me never to trust men or boys. She was so honest and candid with me about the things her uncle did to her from the time she was nine until she was fourteen. She told me all the things to look out for, all the promises these predators would make. The most important thing to remember, she told me, was to never let them think you were a victim because that was when they pounced.

I followed my mom's advice for eight years and I hadn't been so much as hugged the wrong way. I'd kept myself safe, but only by getting myself kicked out of every foster home at the slightest hint that someone might see me as prey. This guy in the beanie doesn't look like a predator, but looks can be deceiving.

He grabs the handle of my backpack and nods toward the stairs. "I'm Chris. I'll take you to your room."

Senia shakes my arm and the living room comes back into focus. "Are you okay?"

I nod quickly and she gives me a tight smile. She knows what just happened, but she's willing to shrug it off because she knows that's exactly what I need tonight. No long talks about getting over the past or seeing a shrink. People have endured far worse than I have. There's devastating famine and wars being waged across the globe. I have nothing to complain about—except the fact that I really don't want to be here tonight.

I spend the entire night hiding my face every time someone I recognize enters the room or explaining how I dropped out because I couldn't pay my student loans. No one here knows the truth. The one smart thing I did last year was drop out before word could spread around campus.

At twenty minutes past midnight, Joanie Tipton finally enters the living room and casts a lazy smile in my direction, and *now* it's time to leave. Joanie is the only person here, besides Senia, who knows why I dropped out. I had to beg Joanie, on my knees, not to tell anybody. It was the second most humiliating moment of my life.

I grab Senia's arm and whisper into her ear, "Don't look now. Mr. Jones just arrived. I have to get out of here."

Mr. Jones is the nickname Senia gave Joanie after she got a chin implant the summer before our sophomore year and we decided she now looks like a transvestite version of Bridget Jones. She even has Renee Zellweger's scrunched eyes. It would be funnier if she didn't hold my secret in her French-manicured hands.

"I'll take you home," she whispers back and I shake my head adamantly.

"No! I'm just going to sleep. You don't need to come home for that. I'll walk."

Her eyebrows furrow and she nods. "Breaking all the rules tonight, huh?" She's referring to the fact that I never walk the streets alone at night. "I know you're sleeping in so I guess I'll see you when I get back on Monday. Love you."

I kiss the top of her head as I rise from the sofa and scoot past her. I glare at Joanie from across the room as I leave, though she isn't looking at me. She's already engaged in a flirtation with a guy who's at least ten years older than us. God, I wish I had a secret on her.

I duck out of the house and pretend to adjust my bangs as I pass a couple making out next to a car in the driveway. The last thing I need is to be recognized as I'm leaving. As soon as I'm out of the couple's line of sight, I pick up my pace. Our apartment is only two and a half blocks away. The only reason Senia drove here is because of her monstrous heels.

I rush out into the crosswalk, eager to get away from the party—and the memories. I don't see the headlights until it's too late.

CHAPTER THREE

Relentless Destiny

THE TIRES SQUEAL, skidding across the asphalt as the truck plunges toward me. I'm frozen as I wait for the impact. I close my eyes and the first and only thought that crosses my mind is that this was inevitable. I'm finally being punished for my sins.

The squealing stops and my nose fills with the stench of burnt rubber. I open my eyes as I feel the heat of the engine against my arm. The grille of the truck is inches away from me and a cloud of smoke surrounds the front of the truck. I hear a car door opening, but I can't see anyone approaching through the smoke until he's right in front of me, Jack Dawson.

"Are you all right?" he asks. I'm shaking with adrenaline, but I don't have a scratch on me. I nod and he grabs my arms. "You look like you're in shock. I should

16

take you to the hospital."

"No!" I shout as I shrug my arms out of his grasp. "I'm fine. I just want to go home."

"I'll take you."

"You almost killed me!"

He lets out a sheepish chuckle and it infuriates me. "Which is why you should let me take you home, so you don't step in front of any more moving vehicles."

"You think it's funny that you almost murdered me?"

"It would have been manslaughter. And, hey, I saved you from that 'roid junkie this morning. I guess this balances that out. Now everything is right with the universe." I curl my lip in disgust and he smiles as he nods toward the cabin of the truck. "Come on. I've already tried to manslaughter you once tonight. I promise I won't try again for at least another twelve hours. You're safe for now."

I roll my eyes as I walk toward the passenger door. He skips after me and opens the door for me to climb in. I step into the truck, using the handgrip to pull myself up, and bounce down into the seat. It smells like the coconut-scented sunblock I've had to purchase by the case since moving to Wrightsville Beach. He shuts the door and I flinch, still jumpy from nearly being mowed down by this monster.

He slides into the driver's seat, but his hands make no move for the ignition. "Why were you running across the street in the middle of the night without looking both ways?"

"I was just walking home from a party. Can we go now?"

"A party? Are you drunk?"

"I don't drink."

He cocks an eyebrow as he studies me, as if his gaze is the equivalent of a Breathalyzer test.

"Hey, I'm not going to sue you, if that's what you're worried about."

"I'm not worried."

Ugh. This guy is annoyingly cocky.

"Let me take you to lunch today to make up for almost killing you."

I turn to look through the rear window of the truck. Where are all the cars? Not that this street is exactly buzzing past midnight, but I'm beginning to think I'm never going to get home if someone doesn't come along and force him out of this intersection.

"I'm sleeping in today."

He tilts his head inquisitively. "What do you mean by sleeping in?"

"I mean curtains drawn, eye mask on, electronic devices switched off. Dead-to-the-world sleeping in," I say as I pull the house keys out of my purse and set the purse on the floor next to my feet.

"Sounds serious."

"Sleep is serious."

"What are you some kind of health nut?"

"I like getting my rest after a night of partying."

"You just said you weren't drinking."

"Are you going to keep asking me questions or are you going to take me home? "Cause I can walk."

He smiles as he turns the key in the ignition and pulls the truck forward. "Cora was right about you," he says, then reaches across the console and shakes my knee.

I slap his hand away, accidentally jabbing him with the keys in my hand. "Hey, there's this thing called personal space. And how do you know Cora?"

"I don't believe in personal space. Separateness is an illusion. We are all connected." He turns to me and flashes me a cunning smile as he pulls into my apartment complex. "Welcome home."

There is only one way he would know where I live and also know Cora.

"You're the new tenant?"

He continues to grin as he guides his truck into the parking space next to Senia's empty space and kills the engine. A million sarcastic remarks about living underneath the person who nearly murdered me whiz through my brain, but I keep them to myself. If there's one thing I hate it's getting on bad terms with a neighbor. Other than the woman I called "Grandma Patty" I didn't really have neighbors growing up in the middle of nowhere with my mom. When I stayed with Senia for a few months after dropping out, I couldn't believe how friendly her family was with their neighbors. They have parties almost every weekend together. Cora has practically become a surrogate grandmother to me. The least I can do is show her new tenant some courtesy.

"Well, then, welcome home to you, too," I say, determined not to let our neighborly relationship get any more awkward.

He glances down at the steering wheel, unimpressed with my attempt at easing the tension. "Don't you want to know what Cora said about you?"

I open the car door and slide out of the truck, letting out a small grunt as I land on the pavement. "Nope. I think I'll let Cora tell me herself. Goodnight…"

"Adam," he says. "I'll tell you my last name at lunch."

I slam the truck door and stomp off toward my front door, which is less than a hundred feet away, right beneath Adam's front door. I'm a few feet away from the door when I hear his truck door slam shut. He's not chasing after me. For some reason I'm both relieved and disappointed by this.

I turn the key in the lock and quickly slip inside before he can reach the staircase leading to his apartment. I slam the front door shut and let out a deep sigh as I lean back against the cool surface of the door. The apartment is stiflingly hot and smells like the day-old muffins I brought home from work this afternoon, but it feels safe.

The knock on the door startles me and I immediately go into defensive-mode. Who the hell does this guy think he is, almost running me over, assuming we're going on a lunch date, then knocking on my door at nearly one a.m.?

I yank open the door, ready to rip him apart, when I see my purse dangling from his finger. I grab it and I'm about to slam the door before I remember Cora. She would be devastated if she knew her new tenant and I were already on bad terms.

Cora's husband died six years ago and her family lives almost three thousand miles away in Idaho. She never leaves the house and her caregiver is a bit standoffish, so her tenants are all she has. The single mom who lived upstairs got remarried and moved out right before I moved in. The upstairs apartment has been empty for four months. Cora must be ecstatic to have a new tenant and some extra income. And I'm ecstatic I won't have to catch her eating cat food straight from the can anymore.

"Thanks," I mutter as he grips the doorway and leans into my personal space, but I hold my ground even though he's making me more uncomfortable than I felt at the party.

"You're welcome, Claire. Can I come in?"

A gust of laughter escapes my lips as I take a step back. "Does that usually work for you?"

He shrugs. "Usually, yes, it does."

"No, you can't come in. I'm going to bed. Goodnight,

Adam."

I push the door closed and he sticks his foot on the threshold to stop it. "I'll be back at two o'clock to take you to lunch. Is that late enough or do you plan on sleeping all afternoon?"

"Goodnight, Adam." *You persistent, sexy little shit!*

I push the door closed and immediately lock the deadbolt. Snatching a bottle of cold water out of the fridge, I drink half of it before I change into an oversized T-shirt and slide under my comforter. I stare at the ceiling for a moment before another memory plays out in front of me like a home movie.

Chris sets my backpack down on the floor in a plain bedroom with a teddy bear wallpaper border. I'm used to sleeping in bedrooms decorated like a toddler's playroom so I don't even flinch.

"My mom wouldn't let me take that stupid border down," he says, lifting his chin toward the ceiling as he digs his hands into the pockets of his jeans.

That's when I see the thin nose ring that dangles from his septum.

"I don't care about the wallpaper. I just want to go to sleep."

His lip quirks up in confusion. "It's three o'clock."

"I haven't slept. I got kicked out last night and I spent the night at the police station. I refuse to sleep in the presence of strangers."

"Afraid someone will shank you in your sleep?"

He smiles and I notice another piercing in his tongue. This guy thinks he's so fucking cool.

"*I'm not having sex with you,*" I declare.

"*What the fuck are you talking about?*"

"*I see the way you're looking at me.*"

"*Yeah, all right. I guess I'll let you sleep and maybe when you wake up you'll chill the fuck out and realize that just because someone's nice to you it doesn't mean they want to fuck you.*"

The shadows on the ceiling blur into darkness. I grab my cell phone and the eye mask from my nightstand, power off the phone, and slide the mask over my head so it rests on my forehead.

I never set my alarm when I'm not working. I cherish the days I get to sleep in. If someone created a religion dedicated to celebrating sleep, I would be the first congregant.

I groan as I turn over in my bed and set the alarm clock on my nightstand to 1 p.m. The things I do for Cora.

CHAPTER FOUR

Relentless Amusement

WHEN I WAKE up, Senia is gone. I never heard her come in while I was sleeping. She's perfected her catlike prowl so as not to wake me up when she comes in late. I take a shower then dress in some skinny jeans and a T-shirt I bought at the surf shop next to the café. I slip on some rubber flip-flops and grab a bottle of water from the fridge just as the first knock comes at the door.

"Coming!" I shout as I grab my purse then guzzle the entire bottle of water.

I open the door and Adam is standing with his back to me, staring at Cora's front door across from mine. Even the back of him is gorgeous. His T-shirt is stretched just a bit taut over his broad shoulders and his skin is so smooth and tanned.

"Where we love is home," he says, reading the wooden

plaque with the chipped blue paint hanging on Cora's door.

"It's a quote," I say as I step outside and pull the door closed. "I gave it to her for her birthday."

"Home that our feet may leave, but not our hearts," he says, finishing the quote. "I knew you'd be awake."

My breath hitches as he turns around and flashes me a soft smile. He looks so good with his sandy-brown hair styled in a calculatedly messy faux-hawk and his lean muscular body towering over me. His hands are tucked into the pockets of his cargo shorts as he gazes at me, waiting for my response.

"Do you read poetry?" I ask, ignoring his infuriating certainty about me being awake and waiting for him.

"When it was required in college, yes. Luckily, I graduated in May, so I'm no longer subject to such cultural annoyances."

"Poetry is a cultural annoyance?"

He smiles because he thinks he's aggravated me. "When do *you* graduate?" he asks, and it seems we're both ignoring each other.

It's an innocent question, but the answer has the possibility of opening up the conversation to more difficult questions. I don't need to tell this guy that I dropped out. He's probably going to take me out to lunch, flirt a little, then try to get into my pants, after which I will tell him to get lost and we'll continue being courteous neighbors who never really speak to each other. Or, maybe, just because he's being nice it doesn't mean he wants to fuck me.

"I don't go to school. I work," I reply, and immediately begin walking to the carports.

He's glued to my side as we cross the driveway toward his truck. "You like poetry and work at a café, but you don't go to school. Are you some kind of struggling artist?"

"You're a nosy little bastard."

He chuckles as he deactivates his car alarm. "It's called getting to know each other. That's what people do on a first date."

He opens the door for me and I look up into his gorgeous green eyes. "This isn't a date. It's a friendly lunch with a neighbor."

"The neighbor who almost killed you," he reminds me. "A little masochistic, don't you think?"

Ugh! What a cocky little shit.

I climb into the truck and look straight ahead, ignoring him until he finally closes the door. I need to meditate, but this guy doesn't know anything about that yet and I'd prefer to keep it that way. Maybe I can just visualize him naked to ease the tension. No, that would definitely not work in this situation.

He slides into the driver's seat and stares at the steering wheel for a second as if he's questioning his approach. "Okay, let's start over. How about we just forget about what happened at the café and what almost happened on the street last night?"

"And what you just said?"

"And what I just said. What do you say? Can we start over?"

His mouth hangs open a little as he awaits my answer and I have to keep myself from imagining what it would be like to suck on his lower lip.

I take a deep breath to clear away this image. "Claire Nixon," I say, holding out my hand.

He takes my hand and immediately brings it to his lips, laying a soft kiss on the backs of my fingers. "Adam Parker, your new neighbor, at your service."

I attempt not to roll my eyes as I pull my hand back, trying to ignore the way my heart is thrumming in my ears. "That's cute."

"I'm serious. Anything you need, I'm happy to help. Leaky faucet, burnt-out light bulb," he pauses to wiggle his eyebrows, "anything at all."

"Wow. You are not predictable at all," I say, reaching for the door handle. "And I've suddenly lost my appetite."

He throws himself across me and grabs my hand. "Wait! I'm sorry. That was out of line. I'm being a total douche. I know. Just give me one more chance. I swear I won't fuck it up."

His hand is on mine and his face is inches away as he leans across my lap. He smells a little minty and a little woodsy as his heat slams into me. I focus on breathing as I watch his eyes skim down my face and land on my mouth.

There's no fighting it as my gaze falls on his lips; those soft, kissable lips he pressed against my hand just a second ago.

"What is your deal?" I ask, sliding my hand out from underneath his. "Why are you so intent on taking me to lunch? I'm fine. You don't need to keep apologizing for nearly running me over."

He sits up and ruffles his hair before he answers. "I actually went to the café yesterday to meet you. I saw you last week when I came to sign the rental agreement. When I asked Cora about you, what she said intrigued me."

"What did she say?"

"I thought you wanted to ask Cora yourself?" I glare at him and he smiles. "She said you were single."

"And?"

"And she said you were the sweetest girl she's ever known."

"And?"

He sighs, looking uncomfortable for once and I'm glad I'm finally able to crack through that smug disposition of his.

"What did she say?" I demand.

"She said you might want to be my friend."

"Be your *friend?*"

"I don't know anybody around here and Cora was concerned that a *quote* "young man like you might get yourself into some trouble without a nice girl around.""

I can't help but smile. That sounds exactly like

something Cora would say. She grew up in Minnesota and is still very old-fashioned about some things. I've only been on one date since I moved into this apartment two and a half months ago. The instant my date brought me home, I glimpsed Cora peeking through her blinds to make sure I wasn't inviting him into my apartment. I love Cora, but she can be a bit nosy and meddlesome.

"So you're just following Cora's advice. Well, let me save you the trouble. I'll go back inside and you can tell Cora that we went out to lunch and had a really nice time. And I'll go back to sleep. Then we all get what we want."

"That's not what I want."

He looks me in the eye and I can't help but marvel at his features: his perfect lips, the straight slope of his nose, the intense glare. He could be on the cover of *GQ* magazine and thousands of girls and guys would drool in the checkout lane.

"What do you want?" I ask, wishing I had brought a bottle of water because my mouth has suddenly gone dry.

"I want to be your friend. And I want to take you to get a fucking burger."

"Well, when you put it that way, how can a girl resist."

He shakes my knee, just the way he did in the truck last night, but this time I don't complain about personal space. This time I kind of like it.

He pulls out of the apartment complex onto Lumina and heads in the direction of Johnnie Mercer's Pier. My body is suddenly zinging with nerves. This feels like a date, but he said he wants to be my friend. I despise uncertainty. I prefer being upfront and honest about everything—except my reasons for dropping out, of course.

A girl is allowed to keep one big secret.

Cora told me this the day I moved in after asking why I had moved all the way to Wrightsville Beach from Raleigh. I told her, jokingly, I'd moved here to see if the ocean could cleanse my sin. That's when she told me, quite seriously, that I was allowed to keep one big secret. For some reason, hearing those words from Cora changed something inside me.

The truth was that I had come to Wrightsville Beach to disappear, possibly forever. After that conversation with Cora, I looked up yoga and meditation studios. Then a customer at the café recommended the female surfer who owned the shop next door. Fallon taught me a few basic meditation techniques and that was it. I was hooked.

When I meditate, I become someone better. I'm not this person who's made a million mistakes; the kind of mistakes that will haunt me for a lifetime. I'm not the person who should be lashed for all the awful, selfish decisions I've made over the last year since *he* left. When I meditate, I'm the new Claire. And today that's who I'll be with Adam.

"You're quiet," he says as he pulls the truck into the pier parking lot.

"Are you taking me to lunch at Buddy's? "Cause I'm allergic to shellfish. I can't even go in there without my throat closing."

"Oh, shit. Sorry. I didn't know that." He looks over his shoulder to see if it's safe to flip a U-turn out of the parking lot. "Where do you want to go?"

"I'm only kidding, but I had Buddy's a couple of days ago. Can we go somewhere else?"

He pulls back out onto Lumina and shakes his head. "Oh, you think that's funny, making me think I'm about to kill you for the second time." I shrug as he turns the truck around and heads back toward our apartment. "All right, jokester, I've got one for you. Why are E.T.'s eyes so big?"

"Duh. Because he saw the phone bill. Please, I've heard that one a billion times."

"Okay, what did the pony say when he had a sore throat?" He pauses for a moment then says, "I apologize. I'm a little horse."

"Are you ten years old?"

He laughs and I can't help but smile as I shake my head. "I've got some better jokes, but I like to start with the clean ones."

"Thanks. I appreciate that."

I want to ask him what he does for a living, but I'm afraid that will lead into what he went to school for. Then that will lead back to why I dropped out. I try to think of a non-standard date question, but my head feels all cloudy just from being near him and I'm having a hard time focusing.

He pulls into our apartment complex a few minutes later and parks his car. "You've probably been to all the restaurants around here a million times. I'm going to make you some lunch."

"Wow. You don't waste any time, do you?"

He throws open his door and glances over his shoulder at me. "I said I wanted to be your friend, Claire. I have no intention of trying to sleep with you."

I'm not sure I totally buy that, but I'll go along with it. I'm starving.

"If this is just a friendly thing, can I invite Cora?" I ask as we cross the driveway.

"You're going to make her walk up all those stairs?"

"Oh, right."

Well, there goes my big plan to use Cora as a buffer. My stomach tightens more with each step and I begin to shiver the moment I see the stairs. He climbs a few steps and turns around when he doesn't hear me behind him.

"Are you coming? I promise to be good." He winks as he says this and I can't believe the nerve of this guy.

What's worse is that I feel drawn to him. I *want* to follow him into his apartment.

"You're not going to poison me, are you?"

"I'm going to poison you with my charm, but only if you keep stalling. Come on."

I take the first step and Chris's voice echoes inside my head.

"I guess I'll let you sleep and maybe when you wake up you'll chill the fuck out and realize that just because someone's nice to you it doesn't mean they want to fuck you. Or you can come downstairs and hang out and maybe I'll play you a song."

I should have gone to sleep that day and I'm beginning to think I should have stayed asleep today.

CHAPTER FIVE

Relentless Questions

MY JAW DROPS the moment we step inside his apartment. The living room looks like the cover of a beach home magazine. One day after moving in and he already has everything in its place, save for a few empty broken-down cardboard boxes in the corner next to a sleek drafting table. His apartment makes our apartment downstairs look like it was designed by six-year-olds.

"Holy shit," I whisper as he makes his way toward the kitchen. "This is amazing."

He smiles as he glances over his shoulder and the dimple on his right cheek quirks up. "I plan on staying here a while."

I follow him into the kitchen and I'm surprised at what he's been able to do with the limited space. He has a fancy stainless-steel refrigerator and his countertops are completely free of clutter. The only items on his counter are a coffee machine and a cordless phone. He pulls something out of a cupboard over the sink and I laugh when I see the box of macaroni and cheese in his hand.

"Is that what you're planning to make?"

"Hey, I never said I could cook. I just said I'd make you lunch. You can't expect me to be good at *everything* or this will never work."

I take a seat on a barstool at the breakfast bar as he begins to prepare our gourmet lunch. "So what else are you good at?"

This is probably a bad question to ask while trapped inside his apartment, but it's safer than asking him what he does for a living.

"Oh, I'm sure you'll figure that out soon enough."

"You know, you don't have to answer every question with a sexual innuendo. I get it."

He fills a pot with some water and places it on the stove. "Let's see… Some would say I'm a good surfer." He's having trouble lighting the burner under the pot.

"Do you need some help?"

I guess he didn't bring his own fancy oven, though I suppose that makes sense if his specialty is mac 'n' cheese. It looks like the same model in our apartment downstairs. I slide off the barstool and join him in the kitchen.

"You probably haven't lit the pilot yet," I say, scooting in next to him.

He smiles down at me. "I can assure you, my pilot is lit."

I roll my eyes as I open the oven door and lift the bottom out. "Do you have a match or a lighter?" He reaches into his pocket and hands me a Zippo. "Do you smoke?" I ask as I reach into the bottom of the oven and light the pilot.

"Sometimes," he admits. "Okay, every night, but only at night."

Probably after sex, I think.

"There you go. Now you can proceed with your culinary masterpiece."

I shut the oven door and hand him back his lighter. His fingers graze my palm as he takes the lighter from me and a chill travels up my arm.

"Thanks. I guess it was your turn to save me."

An image flashes in my mind of a letter tucked away in the top drawer of my nightstand; a letter I've only read once because once was enough. In a single flash I can remember the entire contents of that letter.

DEAR CLAIRE-BEAR:
I'M SORRY.
I WILL LOVE YOU FOREVER
ALWAYS,
YOUR CHRIS

I shake my head, attempting to shake off the guilt, as I scoot around Adam to get back to the barstool.

"I have something I need to tell you," I say, climbing back onto the stool. "I meditate."

"Cool. So do I."

"You do?"

He dumps the dry pasta into the pot before he answers. "Well, sort of. Whenever I'm stressed or if I can't make it to the beach to surf, I'll chill out and do nothing for an hour or so, to clear my head."

"You're not supposed to put the pasta in until the water's boiling."

"Fuck the rules. How often do you meditate?"

I take a deep breath as I prepare to reveal my secret to this almost-stranger. "A lot. Like, a few times a day."

"A few times a day? Do the customers at the café stress you out that much?"

This conversation is not going in a safe direction; might as well push it all the way over the edge.

"Meditation is the way I cope… with the memories."

He looks up from the steaming pot of water and turns to face me. "Go on."

"I'm not going to spill my guts to you," I insist. "I just think you should know about the meditation thing so you don't come banging on my door unannounced."

"Why would I come banging on your door?"

"In the event you should run out of processed cheese, call before you knock."

He finally drains the water from the pot and tosses the powdered cheese and other ingredients in. The pasta makes a gross squishing sound as he stirs it up and I can't believe I'm about to eat mac 'n' cheese on a first date.

I can't believe I'm on a first date.

He grabs two spoons out of a drawer and stabs them into the pot. He sits next to me and places the pot on the breakfast bar between us.

"Bon appétit."

"You really know how to impress a girl, Adam."

He scoops some macaroni onto his spoon and holds it out for me. "I like the way you say my name." I open my mouth and he slowly slides the spoon in. I close my lips around the warm steel and he slowly slides it out. "Look at you. You have that down."

I scoop up some macaroni onto my spoon and he opens his mouth. I bring the spoon a few inches away from his lips before I swoop it away and jam it into my mouth.

"Aw… Claire is greedy," he groans. "That was *my* mac 'n' cheese."

He reaches for my spoon and I pull my hand back. "Nuh-uh."

He doesn't heed my warning and he grabs my wrist with one hand as I attempt to lean back to keep him from reaching the spoon with his other hand.

"I'm hungry," he growls, and I laugh uncontrollably until the stool begins to tilt.

"Oh, shit!" I scream as my stool tips over and we both tumble toward the living-room floor.

He lands on top of me, but he quickly scrambles to his feet and holds out his hand. "Are you okay?" he asks, and there's a definite tinge of worry in his voice.

The carpet burns my elbows as I sit up and grab his hand. He pulls me up until we're standing face to face, our noses inches apart.

"I'm fine," I say, suppressing a chuckle.

He gazes into my eyes, unflinchingly, and I have to look away. "Claire, I find you very, very attractive." I take a step back and hold out my spoon. "I'm not trying to get you into bed. I just wanted to make that known. Since I saw you last week, dancing next to your friend's car, I knew I wanted to get to know you."

I cringe as I realize Adam saw me dancing next to Senia's car when I was imitating what Senia's four-year-old sister does whenever a Justin Bieber song comes on. Then he saw me space out in the café yesterday and, somehow, he still finds me *very, very attractive*.

But I can't shake the nagging voice in my head that tells me Chris would think this was way too soon. Why the fuck should I care what Chris would think? He's the one who left me to go pursue his solo career—even if I did encourage him to leave. I knew it would happen, he was the best rock-blues guitarist I'd ever known, but I guess I never really expected to be left behind. So why the hell should I care what he thinks? He's gone, probably fucking a new groupie every other night, or that Disney celebrity he was seen with three weeks ago.

Ugh! I hate that I even care enough to keep track of this stuff.

"Claire? Where did you go?"

Adam's voice breaks through my troubled thoughts and I push aside that voice in my head that wishes it were Chris calling my name.

"I'm sorry," I mutter. "This is why I meditate. To keep this shit out."

He uprights my barstool and takes a seat on his stool again. He pats the cushioned seat and I pretend not to notice that our knees are touching as I sit down.

"I won't make you eat my gourmet mac if you tell me why you dropped out."

The question shouldn't stun me, but it does. It's like a punch in the chest and I'm suddenly breathless as I try to imagine why Cora would tell him I dropped out.

"Did Cora tell you that?"

He shakes his head adamantly. "I took a guess and you just confirmed it. A smart girl like you doesn't end up working in a small-town café unless she's running away from something. So what is it?"

I rest my arms on the breakfast bar and practically lean

my face into the pot of pasta. "I wish I could tell you."

"It's easy. Just move your jaw and your tongue a little and—*voila!*—out come the words. It's like magic."

I push the pot away and bury my face in my arms. "I wish that were true."

It's true. I really wish I could tell him the truth. I wish I could tell everybody the truth. Keeping the secret alone is enough to make me grind my teeth in my sleep. This secret is eating away at me. The only thing that keeps it from consuming me is meditation.

"Does it have to do with money?"

"No, my tuition was paid for by the State of North Carolina."

"If you tell me why you dropped out, I'll tell you why I moved to Wrightsville Beach," he offers, and he has my attention.

I sit up and look him in the eye. He nods at me as if to say, *The ball's in your court.*

I want to tell him everything, from the day I arrived at the Knight family's house more than five years ago to the day I moved into this apartment almost three months ago, but I can't. Everyone thinks they'll understand, they swear they'll understand, but when you tell them about the horrible things you've done they can't help but judge you or, worse, pity you. I don't want anybody's judgment or pity. I just want to be forgotten and, if I'm lucky enough, forgiven.

"Sorry, but that's a trade I can't make."

He doesn't appear disappointed. He probably anticipated this. "All right. How about this?" He closes his eyes as he takes a beat. "If I can get you to tell me why you dropped out of school then you have to go back."

I chuckle. "That's funny."

"It's not funny. I'm serious. This is a serious bet. I think you desperately want to go back to school and I'm willing to put our *friendship* on the line in order to see that you make it back. What do you say?"

How the hell does he know so much about me from a conversation with Cora? The truth is I do want to go back to school. I was a Sociology major. My dream was to become a caseworker; a better caseworker than the half-dozen I had. I wanted to make sure that no kid felt the way I did, like a nuisance.

I arch my eyebrow and pretend to think about it, because I know he'll never weasel this out of me. "What's in it for me if I don't give up my secret?"

"You get to keep your secret."

"No, you have to do something."

He lets out a deep sigh. "I'll stop stalking you at the café."

"And you'll never try to kill me again?"

"I can't promise that." The sexy smile on his face makes my heart race and, for once, I'm a little worried about the security of my secret.

CHAPTER SIX

Relentless Scheming

CORA JOHNSON CAN take up to twenty minutes to answer her front door. Sometimes she doesn't hear the knocking and other times her joints ache too much to move swiftly. I have a key to her apartment—"In case I croak," she told me, when she handed it over—but I purposely leave it in a drawer in the kitchen. I can't help being a little superstitious, even though life has shown me that there is no order to the universe.

I knock once more and the plaque on the door rattles. The truth is, though I gave Cora the plaque for her birthday, I hoped it would serve as a reminder to me every time I walk out my front door. *Where we love is home.* After eight years of being kicked around, I had a home and people who loved me. Sometimes, I don't know who I miss more, Chris or his mother.

Cora needs to hurry up and answer this door or I'm going to be late for work. I knock again and the door above my head opens. I don't look up, but I can hear Adam's feet tapping the steps as he descends. I cast a sideways glance at the bottom of the staircase, just to watch him from behind as he walks to his car, but he's walking straight toward me.

"Good morning, sunshine. Did you get in some quality meditation time this morning?"

I try not to ogle him as he approaches me looking impossibly fresh and ready to tackle a day at the beach in his gray cargo shorts and Quiksilver tank top, which shows off the defined muscles in his arms.

"I did. I'm just checking in on Cora before I head to work."

"Maybe she's still asleep."

"Cora is up before the sun every day. It takes her a while to answer the door sometimes, but I have to get to work."

He places his hand on my shoulder as his eyebrows furrow. "You look worried. I can check on her for you."

That one sentence coupled with the look of concern and the feeling of his hand on my shoulder takes my breath away. "Really?"

"Yeah, of course. I'll walk you to work and I'll check on her when I get back."

"Walk me to work? I don't need you to do that. I walk to work every day. It's literally four hundred feet away from here."

"I know, but I have to take this stalking gig seriously."

I wish I didn't feel even the slightest bit excited by this, but I am just a girl, and apparently I am easily impressed. Now I'm angry with myself when I should be annoyed with him.

"Fine. Let's go."

I storm off and round the corner toward the front of our little three-apartment complex and quickly make it to the sidewalk on Lumina.

"Where's your friend? I thought you were roommates."

The chill morning air that rolls in from the ocean is slightly briny and I inhale a deep, cleansing breath. The ocean breeze is definitely one of my favorite things about living in Wrightsville.

"She's visiting her parents this weekend. I couldn't go with her because I'm working today."

"Do you always work on the weekend?"

"Pretty much. It's been months since I got the weekend off. I don't really have much else to do and I've got rent to pay."

"Are you working next Saturday? I want to take you somewhere."

"Yes, I'm working both Saturday and Sunday next week."

We're just a few feet away from the café now so he

speeds up to open the door for me.

"Can't you ask for the day off?"

"No, not to go on a date."

"Who said it was a date?" he says with a grin and I roll my eyes.

I stop next to a display of espresso machines and lean in closer so I can whisper. "I can't take a day off. You saw how I screwed up the other day. I've been doing that a lot lately and I *need* this job."

He narrows his eyes as if he's contemplating this information then he nods. "I'll take care of it."

"No! You have to go check on Cora."

I grab fistfuls of his shirt to push him toward the door and he smiles at my feeble attempts to make him move as he stands solidly still.

"All right. Just tell me what I need to check on."

I release his shirt and give him all the details to check for at Cora's: check the cupboards to make sure she hasn't run out of instant oatmeal packets; check the refrigerator for expired foods; make sure the cat hasn't been getting into the trash bins; make sure none of the faucets are left running; and make sure her enormous Maine Coon, Bigfoot, has enough food and water.

"Doesn't she have a caregiver?"

"Tina doesn't get there for another five hours and she's not the most attentive caregiver."

"Got it." He pulls me into a hug so suddenly that my

face smashes against his solid chest and I laugh as I push him away. "That was awkward," he chuckles. "The next one will be better."

I turn my face to hide my uncontrollable grin as I walk behind the café counter.

Linda cocks an eyebrow as I approach. "Who is that tasty young thing? Is that the guy who was in here last week?" she whispers as I pass her on the way to the stockroom to clock in.

I could clock in on the register, but I'm five minutes early and I need that five minutes to wipe this stupid grin off my face.

"I have to clock in," I say, pushing my way through the swinging door.

I sit in the folding metal chair, which Linda refuses to replace with an ergonomic desk chair, and pull my cell phone out of my jeans pocket. I dial Senia's number because, though I know she's still sleeping at 8:55 a.m. on a Sunday, I can't hold in the events of the past day and a half any longer.

She picks up on the second ring. "What?" she groans.

I take a deep breath then spill everything in less than three minutes. When I'm done she's silent.

"Am I crazy?" I ask. "Is this too fast?"

I'm not asking if this is too fast since Chris left, because he left a year ago. She knows what I'm asking and her silence has me twirling my hair nervously.

She clears her throat before she speaks. "Of course it's not too soon. I told you last week, you need to stop being so afraid of people knowing." She clears her throat again and I can hear her taking a sip of water. "Do you need me to fill in for you at the café so you can go on your date?"

I laugh because she doesn't even work at the café, but she probably *could* fill in for me. There is very little Senia can't do. "No. I'll figure something out. I have a week to think of something."

"Let's conspire together, my love," she says, her voice still thick with sleep. "I'm coming home tonight instead of tomorrow. Eddie is getting on my last fucking nerve."

Eddie Goodman, Senia's boyfriend of eight months, nearly drove his car off a cliff when she told him she was moving in with me for the summer. He's possessive as hell and has serious attachment issues, but he's also super hot and shares none of the same classes with Senia—a must for her. She hates dating classmates. When they're not at each other's throats, they're sickeningly adorable together. I call them Enia even though Eddie hates it.

After we hang up, I sit for a minute staring at the computer screen before I clock in two minutes late. Now I have to come up with an excuse for Saturday. When I walk out of the stockroom, Joanne is staring at me from where she stands next to the giant espresso station. Joanne is twenty-two, two years older than I, but she's super timid.

"What's up, Jo?" I ask as I pull my black apron over

my head.

She quickly looks down at the floor. "Nothing. I was just thinking of what I'm going to do on Wednesday."

I tie my apron strings over my lower back and grab a plastic cup to get myself some water. "What are you doing on Wednesday?"

She looks up at me, somewhat confused, as she nervously rubs her dark hair between her fingers. "I have the day off. That guy told me you wanted to switch days off with me. The one you were just talking to."

I shake my head as I realize Adam must have come back in after I disappeared into the stockroom. "You don't have to do that, Jo."

"No, I want to," she says abruptly. "I like working on Saturdays. It's busy."

I suddenly have a feeling that Jo must have her own memories she's trying to bury. "Okay. Thanks."

She smiles and nods as she grabs the plastic cup from my hand and fills it with cold water from the filtered pitcher inside the refrigerator under the counter. She hands the cup back and I'm taken by a sense of concern for her. I wish I knew what it was that made her so shy. Before I can stop myself, I pull her into a hug and I can feel her surprise as she draws in a sharp breath.

"Thanks, Jo."

WHEN I ARRIVE at Cora's house at five after three, I only knock once before the lock turns and the door creaks open. Adam is standing before me wearing a soft smile and I know he's probably been here all day.

"Come on in," he says, holding the door wide open for me.

I walk inside and Cora is sitting in her recliner in front of the television with Bigfoot in her lap. The apartment is clean and the usual sharp litter box smell is gone. Cora looks up and smiles so big I can see the gap where she's missing her two back molars.

"Hello, honey. Have you met Adam Parker? He's your new neighbor," she says in a voice that makes me feel a little like a preschooler being introduced to a classmate. "I think you two should get to know each other."

She obviously doesn't know about our date yet.

Adam takes a seat on the sofa, on the side closest to the recliner, and pats the cushion next to him. "Yeah, come sit down, Claire. Let's get to know each other."

I take a seat on the sofa, making sure to put at least a foot of space between Adam and me.

"What did you do today? Where's Tina?" I ask as I turn to Cora.

"Adam's been taking care of me today. He gave her the day off," she says, her eyes crinkling with delight.

I narrow my eyes at him and he grabs Cora's hand as

he turns back to her. "It was my pleasure. I didn't have anything to do today since the only other person I know in this town was working."

"You work too much, Claire," Cora chimes in as she continues to stroke Bigfoot with her free hand.

Geez. It's like these two have spent the past six hours scheming to get Adam and me together. First he switches my schedule without my knowledge and now he's using Cora to get on my good side. He is a master conspirator.

I stand up and do a quick check around the kitchen just to satisfy my curiosity. As expected, he did everything I asked. He even stocked her cupboard with plenty of hot cereal packets and her refrigerator with lots of fresh fruit.

"Well, it looks like you're all taken care of so I'm going to head home," I say as I plant a kiss on Cora's forehead and rub Bigfoot's head. "I need to shower and get to bed early. I have the early shift tomorrow."

"Walk her home, Adam," she says sweetly and he immediately pops up off the sofa.

"See you later, Cora. We'll have to watch that movie another time."

"See you later, sonny," she says, and I know what's coming next. "But just because I call you sonny, doesn't mean you're bright."

He laughs and points at her. "I can't keep up with you, C."

Adam follows me out of the apartment and uses his

own key, which Cora must have given him, to lock her deadbolt.

I take a few steps and turn around when I reach my door. "*C?* Did you spend the whole day with her?"

"I ran a few errands for her, but other than that, yes, I spent the day with Cora. She's funny and we were about to watch a movie before you interrupted us."

"Oh, well, don't let me interrupt your date with Cora. Please, go right back in."

He steps forward and my back hits my front door as I take a step back. He leans against the door with his hands on either side of my head, effectively caging me in.

"Are you jealous of my relationship with Cora?"

His breath is hot against my nose and warmth rushes through me, lighting up my core.

"I just don't want her to get used to having you around. She's had a lot of people bail on her and I…" His face is getting closer with every word I speak. "I don't want her to get hurt."

"Are you sure we're talking about Cora?" he whispers against my lips, lingering for a moment before he pushes away from the door. "I work all week, but I'll be by your house at nine a.m. on Saturday. Wear a bathing suit under your clothes."

I let out a deep sigh and scramble into my apartment, slamming the door behind me. I take a few calming breaths, trying to ignore the ache pulsating between my legs as I make my way toward the bedroom to meditate.

CHAPTER SEVEN

Relentless Games

I DON'T HEAR from Adam all week. And, although I do hear him coming in and out of his apartment a few times, he never stops by to say hi. But I know he's still visiting Cora because every time I pop in on her, she's always wearing an enormous grin. When Senia and I arrive at her house on Friday evening at seven, Tina answers the door.

"Oh, hi, Claire," she says in an exasperated tone.

She quickly waddles into the kitchen to continue washing the dinner dishes. I try not to get upset with Tina. That's just her manner. She's never been particularly friendly and I've never taken the time to get to know her enough to find out why.

I step inside with Senia and find Adam and Cora engaged in a game of cards on a wooden TV tray table. Neither of them look up from their cards. I know he said he was going to be working all week, but it's not as if he couldn't just drop by and say hello—at least pretend I exist. The fact that I neglected to ask him what he does for a living just made the entire week of waiting even more uncomfortable. When Senia and I discussed it, our best guess was he changed his mind about the date and couldn't bring himself to break the news to me.

"We'll come by later," I say, turning to head out the open front door.

Senia grabs my arm to stop me. "No, we can't. Or at least, I can't. Eddie's coming over."

I wrestle my arm out of her firm grip and Cora finally looks up at me from her cards. "Oh, hi, honey. I didn't see you there. Want to get in on this action?"

Adam smiles, but he still doesn't look at me. What is his problem? My stomach is in knots and I feel like a total idiot for allowing myself to think that a guy like him could be interested in me.

"What's your problem?" Senia asks and Adam finally looks up.

"Senia, please don't do this. Come on. Let's go home." I try to pull her toward the door, but she's four inches taller and at least fifteen pounds heavier than I. She's not budging.

"I'm sorry. Are you talking to me?"

To his credit, Adam looks genuinely confused. Maybe he's a professional actor.

"Don't pretend you don't know what I'm talking about. You left Claire hanging all week wondering if you two were still hanging out tomorrow and now you ignore her. What kind of asshole does something like that?" She turns to Cora, whose mouth is hanging open. "Sorry, Cora."

"Is this true, Adam?" Cora asks, laying her cards on the TV table face-up.

Adam lays his cards down and looks straight at me. "I didn't visit you during the week because I was working."

Senia shakes her head. "We heard you coming and going from your apartment."

He turns on Senia. "You didn't let me finish."

She crosses her arms. "Go ahead."

"I was working, and when I'm working I'm usually in a shitty mood. I didn't want you to see me like that so I just stayed away."

"That doesn't explain why you ignored me when we came in here," I say, and he turns to me with what I know is an apology ready to roll off his tongue.

"That was just bad manners," he says, and a tiny smile curls the corners of his lips. "Cora's a sneaky one. I have to keep my eyes on her at all times when we're playing cards."

If this guy is any fucking sweeter I'm going to need a dentist. I can't even be angry that he's moving in on my turf because he seems to be doing a better job than me at keeping Cora company.

I turn to Senia and she raises her eyebrows as if to say,

You're on your own.

She claps me on the shoulder and heads for the door. "I have to go wait for Eddie. Don't want him to accuse me of getting too friendly with the new neighbor."

"Sit down, honey," Adam says, using Cora's favorite term of endearment as I shut the front door behind Senia.

When I turn around, he's rubbing the cushion next to him and wearing a sexy smile. I don't know if I'd rather punch him or kiss him.

"I'm not your honey," I mutter as I sit next to him.

He drapes his arm around my shoulder and presses his lips softly against my temple. I'm frozen as my shoulders and arms go weak.

His lips are warm against my cheek as they travel to my ear. "Just play along. I told her we were going on a date and it made her so fucking happy."

I shake my head and turn to face him. "You think you're so clever, using Cora to get to me."

He shrugs, keeping his eyes on me as he reaches for the cards on the table. "Can you blame me for wanting to keep her happy?"

"Adam, honey, I feel like I've been hit by a truck and run over twice," Cora says as she shoos Bigfoot off her lap. Bigfoot immediately scurries towards me to rub his fluffy body against my bare legs. "I'll have to finish embarrassing you tomorrow. Can you lock up on your way out?"

Adam quickly gets to his feet to help Cora out of the

recliner. "Of course, right after I help Tina clean up."

I watch in awe as he guides Cora to her room, followed closely by Tina. I spring up from the sofa and make my way into the kitchen to finish doing the dishes. I grab a pot with a little left-over chicken soup and dump the contents down the drain before hitting the switch on the garbage disposal. A few bits of carrot stick to the sides of the steel sink and I push them into the drain with my hand. I listen to the sound as they hit the blades inside the garbage disposal, so lost in the squishy, grinding noise that I jump when Adam appears at my side.

"You scare easily," he says as he flips the switch on the garbage disposal and the grinding noise dies.

I wipe down the sink one last time before I turn to face him. "Thanks for hanging out with her."

I step sideways to get around him and he steps sideways to block me. "I know our date isn't until tomorrow, but what are you doing tonight?"

I stare at his chin to avoid staring at his mouth or eyes. "Probably watching Senia's boyfriend get drunk. Then I'll be listening to their wall-banging from the safety of the sofa."

He tilts his head as he considers this information. "You're welcome to hang out with me tonight, you know, if you need to escape."

Tina walks in before I can answer. "She's down for the count," she says, snatching her tan leather purse off the kitchen counter. "I'll see you *two* on Monday."

She appears peeved that Cora now has two companions around to keep her from slacking off. Once she closes the door behind her, I slither around Adam and dart toward the door. He quickly follows and hooks his arm around my waist.

"Hey!" I whisper-shout at him over my shoulder. "Personal space!"

He grabs the sides of my waist and turns me around so we're facing each other. "We're beyond that, honey." He chuckles softly and I cringe at his arrogance. "I'm kidding. Go ahead and get whatever you need for the night. You can sleep in my bed and I'll sleep on the sofa. I know how important it is that you get your sleep." I narrow my eyes at him and he laughs again. "What? I'm just trying to help. I swear I'll keep my hands to myself."

It's a very tempting offer. I won't get to sleep until three or four in the morning or whatever God-forsaken hour Senia and Eddie tire out. Of course, I hardly know this guy other than the fact that he's extremely patient and charming, and more than a bit persistent. He doesn't strike me as the kind of guy who would force himself on me. Plus, it will be convenient not to have to wake up Senia and Eddie when I get ready for our date tomorrow morning.

"Fine, but if you think you're getting laid you're going to be very disappointed. And if you try anything funny, I'm leaving and our date is off. Got it?"

He clasps his hands behind his back. "I wouldn't dream of jeopardizing all the fun we're going to have on our date."

I toss my toothbrush and a few cleansing products into my makeup bag. The makeup bag gets thrown into my Roxy backpack with my bikini, a beach dress, and some gladiator sandals. When I come out of the bedroom, Senia is glaring at me from the other side of the breakfast bar.

"You going somewhere?"

"I'm going to hang out at Adam's tonight so you and Eddie can be alone. We're leaving early in the morning for whatever he has planned. I don't want to wake you up getting ready."

"You're spending the night with him?"

"Not with him, just in his bed. He's sleeping on the sofa."

Saying the words aloud makes it sound so much worse than it sounded when I agreed to this five minutes ago with Adam breathing on my face.

"Claire, this is *so* not like you," she says, rounding the breakfast bar toward me. "I love it!" She smiles hugely, showing off all her perfectly white teeth, then throws her arms around my shoulders. "I'm so proud of you."

I pat her back a few times and she finally lets go. "This is not a big deal. We're just hanging out. I am *not* sleeping with him."

"I know. But it's a start." She kisses my forehead

before I leave.

My heart pulses in every inch of my body as I climb the steps to Adam's apartment. My feet are like concrete blocks attached to my legs as I grip the handrail and drag myself up the final step and stand before apartment B. I roll my shoulders in an attempt to loosen the tension then take a deep breath and knock.

He answers the door immediately, as if he were standing on the other side impatiently waiting and watching through the peephole. The smile on his face makes my stomach flutter. He looks genuinely excited and somewhat relieved, as if he thought I might change my mind.

"Welcome back," he says, waving me inside.

The lamps are lit inside his dazzling apartment, bathing the space in a warm glow. Everything is still perfectly clean. The LCD TV affixed to the wall is set to MTV, but the volume is too low to hear. Nothing out of place—except maybe me.

"Can you change that?" I say, pointing at the TV. "I hate MTV."

"You and I are not going to get along," he says, closing the front door.

I don't need to tell him the reason I've avoided watching MTV for nearly a year. I'm here to get past that, not to dwell on it.

He snatches the remote from the black coffee table and changes it to the Discovery Channel. "Better?"

I nod and set my backpack on the floor next to the sofa. He immediately slides past me and snatches it up. "I'll put that in the bedroom for you. Want to come see your room at Hotel Parker?"

"So hospitable," I say as I follow him toward a dark hallway.

The hallway is short, just like our apartment downstairs, and he quickly flips the light switch as we enter his bedroom. He sets my bag down on the king-sized bed as I look around. As expected, his room is pretty enough to be a suite in a modern hotel.

"How much is this going to cost me?" I ask.

He shakes his head. "Please don't say stuff like that. There's only so much teasing I can resist."

It feels good to be able to joke around with him like this. It means I feel safe.

"We'd better go watch some Discovery Channel," I suggest, and he nods. Yes, watching TV is safer than standing in his bedroom.

After twenty minutes of me silently swooning over Bear Grylls and him pointing out that Bear's cameraman is the real hero of the show, he turns off the TV and looks at me.

"All right. It's time to play a game," he declares. "Question tennis. I ask you a question and you answer with a question, but it has to be relevant to what I asked. If you break the rhythm by not asking a question then you have to answer one question truthfully before the game can continue. Are you ready?"

"Leave it to you to find a game that allows you *not* to answer questions."

"You are being afforded that same luxury, missy, so stop complaining. Okay, you go first."

I pull my legs up onto the sofa and sit cross-legged as I face him. "What do you do for a living?"

"Does it really matter?"

"Does it really put you in a shitty mood?"

"Does that concern you?"

"It's a simple question."

"Ah-ha!" he shouts, pointing at me. "You messed up. Now you have to answer a question."

I know what he's going to ask, but I'm not the least bit worried because there's no way I'm going to tell him just to comply with a stupid game.

"Go ahead."

He smiles as he leans back against the arm of the sofa. "When did your last relationship end?"

This isn't the question I expected, but I've come to realize that Adam rarely does anything I expect him to do.

I fidget with the loose threads of my cutoff shorts. "It ended almost exactly one year ago."

"Why?"

"Nuh-uh. You got your answer. Now back to the game."

"If you tell me why then I'll tell you where I work."

"That's not an even trade."

He leans forward. "I work for my dad. He owns a construction company in Wilmington. The company's been in the family for more than a hundred years so it's pretty much expected that I'm going to take over once my dad retires in a few years. I fucking hate it."

His green eyes appear darker, harder, as he stares at me and I can see that it upsets him just to talk about this. I know he's waiting for me now, but all I can think of is how much I want to give him a hug. I want to tell him how well I know the fear of disappointing others. I want to tell him how familiar I am with the guilt that comes from making selfish decisions.

"My ex was offered his dream job and I was starting my sophomore year at UNC. He was going to be doing a lot of traveling, so I decided it would be best to break up so he could experience this new opportunity to the fullest. I didn't want to weigh him down the way I had for more than four years."

"Four years? So he was your first love?"

The muscles in my chest tighten at these two words. Chris was more than my first love. He was my first friend, my first family, my first heartbreak, and my deepest betrayal.

I nod as I inhale a deep breath. "I'm tired. I think I should go to bed."

He nods solemnly. "You know where the bathroom is

if you need to do any girly stuff. Feel free to pilfer my toiletries."

I smile at his attempt to ease the tension then make my way to the bedroom to grab my makeup bag. As I pull it out of my backpack, a wave of nausea rolls through me. I sit on the bed to ride it out as sweat beads on my forehead. Hugging myself, I breathe deeply and close my eyes, trying to focus on something, anything, other than the pain of losing everything.

The creaky floor alerts me to Adam's presence. I open my eyes to find him standing in the doorway.

"Do you need to meditate or do you need some company?"

"Can I answer that question with a question?" He nods and I draw in a shaky breath. "Can you stay with me tonight?"

He steps inside and slides onto the bed behind me. I look over my shoulder at him as he laces his fingers behind his head and lies back on the pillow.

"My hands will stay here all night or you have permission to post a video of me dancing to Justin Bieber on YouTube."

I toss my makeup bag onto the floor and lie back on the pillow next to him. "Tell me a joke."

He reaches toward the nightstand and turns off the lamp. For once, the darkness is comforting. I can pretend I'm talking to anyone.

"Corny or dirty?" he asks, settling back onto his pillow.

"Dirty," I say, grateful that he can't see my smile through the darkness.

He lets out a tiny huff of laughter. "Man, you are going to regret saying that." He pauses a moment before he says, "When is an elf not an elf?"

"When?"

"When she's sucking dick. Then she's a goblin."

I let loose a quick chuckle. "That's corny, but still kind of funny."

"You deserve the best of both worlds."

The silence that follows his comment is painful. Finally, I turn onto my side to face him. The soft glow of the streetlamp shines through his curtains, outlining the silhouette of his perfect nose and lips. He turns to me and I can just barely glimpse his smile through the darkness.

"Maybe we should go to sleep now," I whisper, my voice sounding somewhat strangled by the power of his presence.

"Yeah, we have to get up early." He moves to get up and I grab his arm.

"You don't have to go."

He slowly settles back onto the bed, a little closer to me than he was before. I can feel the heat of his shoulder next to my face. He lifts his arm and I realize he's inviting me to cuddle with him. My heart pounds as I scoot toward him, drape my arm over his chest, and lay my head on his solid shoulder. He wraps his arm around me and gives my shoulder a light squeeze.

"Sweet dreams, Claire."

"Goodnight, Adam."

CHAPTER EIGHT

Relentless Competition

I WAKE WITH Adam's gray T-shirt clenched in my fist and a large crack of summer sunrise illuminating the humid air in the bedroom. His chest is hot and steamy against my cheek as it rises and falls slowly beneath me. I hold my breath as I slowly loosen my grip on his shirt. He lets out a soft grunt and I freeze.

I take in a measured breath as I move my hand, slower this time. The moment I begin to lift my head he shifts his weight, tightening his grip on my shoulder. It can't be that early and he did say we were leaving at nine.

Ah, fuck it.

I push off his chest to sit up. His eyebrows scrunch up as he opens his eyes. "What time is it?"

"I don't know, but you said we were leaving early so I figured we should probably get up and get ready."

He squints at me through the hazy morning light and my breath catches in my throat. He looks way too adorable with his hair sticking out in million different directions.

"Well, aren't you a vision in the morning," he says, with a sly grin.

I reach up and feel my hair plastered to the right side of my head with sweat. The left side is sticking out several inches. I start to smooth it down and he yanks me down on top of him, ruffling my hair some more.

"Hey!" I squeal as I wrestle myself from his grip.

He laughs as he sits up and makes his way to the window to open the blinds just enough so the light penetrates the curtains, washing everything in the room, including him, in a creamy glow.

"You can take a shower first. I'll make you some breakfast while you wash up."

"Mac 'n' cheese again?" I say as I slide off the bed and grab the purple makeup bag I tossed onto the floor last night.

"You should be so lucky. Nah, just a plain, old smoothie this time. We're gonna eat some kickass barbecue later. You're not a vegetarian, are you?"

"I love animals," I reply solemnly. "Especially when they're cooked."

He chuckles as he walks past me and I'm struck by how comfortable I feel here, like sleeping over at my hot neighbor's house is something I do often. Does this make me a slut? No, we haven't even kissed yet. Most people would have kissed by now. Is that a bad sign?

"Hey, just a heads-up," I say as I come out of the bedroom, stopping in front of the bathroom door. "I'm probably going to meditate in there, but I promise I'll make it quick."

"You can meditate out here. We can do it together."

"Really?"

"Yeah, I'll put some extra roofies in your smoothie to help you relax."

"Aw... that's so thoughtful."

He shrugs modestly and I have to keep myself from sighing at how cute he looks. "Like I said before, only the best for Claire."

I shake my head as I enter the bathroom, which looks just like our bathroom downstairs. I take a quick shower, thanking myself for remembering to bring my own body wash and shampoo when I see his man-scented bath products. After I brush my teeth and hair and put my bikini on underneath my dress, I exit the bathroom to find him sitting cross-legged on the rug in the living room. The coffee table has been pushed aside to make room for us and he's wearing a serene smile.

I set my makeup bag on the breakfast bar and place my hands on my knees as I sit across from him. "I'm going to picture the ocean. You don't have to tell me what you're going to meditate on."

"I wasn't planning to tell you," he replies.

"Good because I don't want to know."

"I'm sure you can guess, though."

"I'm sure I can, but I won't."

I shake my head as I take a deep breath, ignoring the sexy grin on his face as I close my eyes. I expel the breath slowly and imagine that all my worries about Chris and college are being pushed out at the same time. Drawing in another deep breath, I imagine standing on the beach, breathing in the salty air as the ocean waves roll in. I breathe out and focus my attention on a sailboat floating on the distant surface of the ocean. The jagged silhouette of the boat bobs against the skyline and I imagine the motion of the water carrying me out to sea on that boat, so far that I can no longer see the shore. I lie back on the deck of the boat and gaze at the blue sky above me. The clouds swirl in and out of view behind the giant sails. I close my eyes and allow the boat to rock me gently, swaying and pitching softly up and down as my tension melts away.

I open my eyes and Adam's eyes are still closed. I wait a moment until his eyelids flutter open and he lets out a deep sigh.

"Man, that feels good. I can see why you're addicted to this."

"I've never meditated with anyone other than Fallon, and that was only a couple of times. This is different, but cool."

He shakes his head as he looks at the floor between us. "Okay, I lied. I didn't meditate. I stared at you the whole time." He reaches across the space between us and grabs my hand. "But it did feel good."

"You're such a sleaze," I say, smacking his hand away. "Go take a shower."

He takes a quick shower, makes us each a strawberry-banana smoothie, and we're out the door within thirty minutes.

We're walking down the steps outside his apartment when I have a mini-epiphany. "Wait a minute. You work at a construction company and you don't know how to light a pilot on a stove?"

I glance over my shoulder and he grins sheepishly. "I wanted to give you a chance to show off."

"How generous," I mutter as we reach the landing and I set off toward his truck.

He grabs my hand and I'm yanked backward. "We're walking to the beach."

"You're taking me to the surf tournament?"

"The Summer Swell Pro-Am. It's the only one in this area and it's today."

"Where's your surfboard?" I ask, when we reach the sidewalk.

I don't bother to mention that he's still holding my hand and just as this thought crosses my mind he threads his fingers through mine.

"I'm not surfing. Today we're watching the pros."

We make it to the corner of Charlotte and Lumina and I'm suddenly aware of all the pedestrians on their way to the tournament. I'm hyperaware that Adam and I must look like a couple. I hit pause on my love life so many months ago; I almost forgot what it feels like to be a couple in public. Girls in short shorts pass us as we cross the street and some of them make no attempt to hide their ogling. I glance up at Adam to see if maybe he's egging them on, but his gaze is fixed straight ahead to where Charlotte opens onto the beach.

The street is packed with tourists in shorts and visors and, with no sidewalks, they all roam through the middle of Charlotte Street laughing and talking among themselves. When we reach the sand, I glimpse the bleachers constructed on the beach. Off in the distance, I see a stage where people are already squeezing in against the platform as sound equipment and instruments are set up for a concert. The briny smell of the ocean hits me as a breeze sweeps over us, lifting the hairs that hang loose from my ponytail and making my skin prickle. The sand is warm on the surface but cool when my feet sink down. I haven't been to the beach in a couple of weeks and I always avoid it during big events like this.

My hand is getting sweaty. I feel an intense urge to let go of Adam's hand to wipe the sweat on my hip, but I don't. Being uncomfortable is part of being on a date, right?

Like holding in your farts when you're in a new relationship. It's a necessary evil. Suddenly, I think of the first time I farted in front of Chris and I can't help but smile.

"Why are you so happy?" Adam asks as we trudge across the sand toward the bleachers.

"I'm thinking of how sweaty my hand feels right now."

He grips my hand tighter. "Too bad. I'm not letting go."

"I'll never let go, Jack," I whisper dramatically, and he shakes his head.

"You jump, I jump," he replies, and I laugh.

"You love *Titanic*," I tease him. "You know, that first day I saw you in the café, I kept calling you Jack Dawson in my head."

"Do I look that old to you?"

"No, and you're much better looking than him, anyway."

"You'd better watch out, Claire," he says as we climb the steel steps up to the bleachers. "If you keep saying stuff like that I'm going to be forced to take you into the water for a swimming lesson."

"I know what that means and I would never. There are a million people out here."

We sit at the end of a bench a few rows down from the top and the steel bench is hot against the backs of my legs.

He finally lets go of my hand and leans over to whisper

in my ear. "I thought you liked taking risks."

His lips linger against my ear and his breath sends a tingling sensation racing through me. I swallow hard as I shift in my seat and he finally pulls away.

"The first group hits the water in a few minutes," he says, as if I care. "So we have some time to finish our little game of questions. But this time we have to actually answer. No answering a question with a question." He grabs my hand again before he begins. "What's your favorite time of day?"

I pause for a minute to think, though I already know the answer. "That time of day when the sun hasn't come up yet, but you can already feel it coming. It's an elusive warmth, like a subtle promise whispered in your ear and you can go on with your day knowing you've been given another chance to get it right. Sometimes I get up early just so I can sit outside with a cup of tea and feel it."

I turn to Adam and his face is serious. "I know it's a total cliché, but my favorite time of day is sunset." He takes a deep breath then turns his gaze to the water. "We used to live near Carolina Beach and my dad would take me out every day after school to surf until the sun went down. It's bittersweet because the sunset always made me a little sad knowing that it was the signal for us to leave—and I never wanted to leave the water. But it also brings back some really good feelings about that time in my life, you know, before things got complicated."

There's so much I want to ask him now, but I have to pick just one question.

"Okay, why do you still work for your dad if you hate it? And don't give me the obvious answer of family obligation because you don't strike me as the kind of guy who would let that stop him from doing anything."

He leans forward, resting his elbows on the tops of his legs and I'm forced to lean forward with him since he's still gripping my hand like a life raft.

He encapsulates my hand in both of his and my hand disappears. "I guess we both have some questions we're not ready to answer."

I wait a moment before I nudge his shoulder for him to look up. "Hey, the first group just paddled out."

During the entire first round, and half the second round, Adam explains the rules of the tournament and what each surfer needs to score to move on. Every time one of them executes a difficult trick without bailing Adam gets so excited and cheers with the crowd. His enthusiasm is infectious and before long, I find myself cheering so loudly my throat aches by the end of the second round. I haven't had this much fun on a date since… well, I don't know if I've *ever* had this much fun on a date.

As we're sitting there waiting for the third round to begin, a group of guys in board shorts with beads of water and sand sparkling on their shirtless chests pass us on the way up to the next row of bleachers. A couple of them ogle me as they pass and Adam's grip tightens on my hand. I look at him and the tiny muscle in his jaw is twitching.

"Come on. Let's go down and watch some of the bands while we wait for the next round."

I allow him to pull me along down the bleachers to the sand and toward the stage before I say anything. "What was that about?"

"What?"

"That?" I say, nodding toward the bleachers behind us. "You're not upset about those guys checking me out, are you?"

He grits his teeth again as he lets out a breath through his nostrils. "I don't like... Wait, let me rephrase that. I sometimes have a problem controlling my temper. That's part of the reason I moved here. I've learned that the only way for me to deal with it is to avoid situations that set me off."

Great. I had to find the one sweet guy in Wrightsville Beach with anger issues. I realize quite abruptly that we've both let go of each other's hands as we approach the crowd huddled around the stage where a DJ is now playing electronic dance music. Some people jump up and down to the beat while others writhe against each other. Some hold cans of soda in their hands, which, by the enthusiasm of their thrusts, are probably filled with more than carbonated water and high-fructose corn syrup.

The smell of a dozen different sunscreens, coconut,

pineapple, jasmine, combined with the scent of hot, sweaty bodies grinding against each other is intoxicating. I follow Adam as he moves through the crowd, parting the swaying sea of bodies for me. He makes it as close as a few rows of bodies from the stage before he turns around, wraps his arms around my waist, and lifts me up.

I try not to giggle as I get a swooping sensation in my belly. I can feel my dress riding up my back, exposing my bikini bottoms to everyone. I wrap my arms around his neck as he leans his forehead against mine.

"Claire," he says, just loud enough so I can hear him over the music. "I'm going to kiss you."

His breath is hot against my mouth as he slowly moves in, stopping just before our lips touch and my whole body aches for this kiss. He smiles and I pull him toward me, but he turns his head at the last second and my lips brush his cheek.

"But not here," he says into my ear, and I'm furious with frustration.

"Put me down."

He plants a soft kiss on my cheekbone then laughs when I wipe it away. He finally sets me down on the sand, but he holds onto my waist so I can't turn away.

"Don't be mad," he yells over the music. "I just want it to be perfect, like you."

I roll my eyes. "Boy, you've got a rude awakening coming if you think I'm perfect."

"You're perfect," he insists as he grabs my face and forces me to look him in the eye. "Just the right amount of flaws."

Our chests heave against each other and I can't take it anymore. "I want to go home."

"So soon?"

"You didn't let me finish," I say, making no attempt to keep myself from staring at his gorgeous lips. "I want to go home… with you."

CHAPTER NINE

Relentless Desire

WE HALF-RUN AND half-walk back to his apartment. The entire time I'm trying to mentally shutdown all the alarm bells going off inside my brain. This guy is trouble. He pursues me to the point that I'm begging *him* to go to bed with him. Plus, he's admitted to having rage issues. This is wrong, wrong, wrong.

So why does it feel so damn right?

As soon as he closes his front door, he clasps his hand around the back of my neck, ensnaring a handful of my hair, and pulls my face toward him. His first kiss is soft as he presses his lips to the corner of my mouth. He kisses the other corner and a sigh builds inside my chest. His tongue parts my lips and I whimper as my body melts into him, too weak to fight it.

As if he could sense this, he scoops me up in his arms

and carries me to his bedroom. He lays me down on the bed and his gaze slides over me as if I'm a meal he's preparing to devour and he can't decide where to start.

He reaches behind his back and turns on an oscillating fan without breaking eye contact with me. "It's *very* hot in here."

He pulls off his tank top and lies on top of me, supporting his weight on his hands as he softly kisses my forehead. "I want to make love to you," he whispers as his lips brush my temple and leave a burning trail down the side of my face before he reaches my ear. "I want to leave you dazed and confused for a week with nothing but my name on your lips."

I'm fading fast. One part of me wants him to keep going, but another voice inside me keeps screaming that this is wrong. I'm falling too fast. It's going to happen again.

I need to quiet that voice.

I clutch his hair and pull his face away from my neck. "Tell me a joke. Quick." He smiles as he leans down to kiss me and, as his tongue slides over mine, a clash of emotions threatens to rip me in half. "Please," I beg, and he groans into my mouth.

"Claire, didn't anyone ever warn you to never trust an atom?" He kisses the corner of my mouth so softly it sends a gust of longing sweeping through me. "They make everything up."

His fingers skim the side of my thigh as they travel

upward, snagging the hem of my dress and exposing my skin to the cool air of the fan.

My breath hitches as his fingers toy with the edge of my bikini bottoms. "Adam, did anyone ever tell you your jokes are bad and you should feel bad?"

"Never," he whispers as he presses his lips against the swell of my breast.

His hand slides between my thighs and I gasp as he strokes me through the fabric of my bikini.

"Is this your subtle way of telling me I shouldn't trust you?" I say, eager to fill my brain with any thought other than the voice that keeps telling me to stop.

His hand slides up to my belly then beneath the waistband of my bikini bottoms. My whole body goes rigid.

"Is this okay?" he asks, looking into my eyes as his fingers come to rest on my swollen flesh.

I want to tell him it is more than okay. I desperately want him to keep going. I want to feel him inside me. I want to release all this tension we've built up on the beach and over the past week. But I keep thinking about the day my life changed one year ago and the events—the mistakes—that led to that day. And the countless lies I've told since then.

I push him off me and sit up on the bed. "I can't. I'm sorry."

I bury my face in my knees and he lets out a frustrated sigh as he sits up. "Hey," he murmurs as he lifts my chin.

"I'm not irritated with you, if that's what you think."

I purse my lips, unconvinced, as I lay my cheek against my knee. "You should take this opportunity to run as far away from me as you can."

He lays his palm on the side of my face and strokes my cheekbone with his thumb. "You're not getting rid of me that easily. You still owe me something." He sweeps my hair over my shoulder then lightly traces a heart on my back.

I close my eyes as he slides over to sit behind me. His legs stretch out on either side of my hips as he rubs my shoulders. I keep my eyes tightly shut as I try to ignore the tingling between my legs when his hand touches my butt as he adjusts his crotch.

"I'm… I'm thirsty. It's really hot in here."

He kisses the back of my neck before he scoots off the bed. "I'll get you some water."

As he walks out of the bedroom, Jo pops into my head. I wouldn't have the day off today if it weren't for her willing to switch shifts with me. I should go thank her again. No, I'm just looking for an excuse to get out of this apartment.

I tap my foot on the mattress as I wait impatiently, but after ten minutes I begin to worry. Then the smell of smoke makes my nose perk up and my body tense.

I scramble off the bed and slip on my flip-flops before I head out to the kitchen. Adam is standing in the kitchen blowing smoke out through the window above the sink. He holds a plastic blue bong in his right hand and a lighter in his left. I walk into the kitchen and he smiles at me.

"Sorry, I should have brought the water first. It's right there." He nods toward a tall glass of ice water on the counter, but I don't pick it up.

He's a pothead. That's what he smokes every night.

He sets the bong and the lighter down on the counter and I glimpse a tattoo on the left side of his chest: *Ride it out.* The letters are written in dripping block text beneath a tattoo of a compass. The inner part of the compass is filled with brilliant blue waves. The water is his compass. I want to touch it, but I'm too peeved by the fact that he's a pothead.

"I should go," I say as I turn toward the door and, as expected, he grabs my hand.

"Hey, are you pissed that I didn't bring your water or that I'm smoking?"

"Neither," I say, without looking at him.

He reaches up and turns my face toward him. Even through the haze of smoke in the kitchen, he still looks beautiful.

"Don't go."

I close my eyes to block out the sight of his perfect lips and the slight pinkness in the whites of his eyes.

"I'm sorry, this is going to sound totally lame, but I can't date a pothead. My mom died of a drug overdose. And I know weed is nothing like heroin, but I promised myself a long time ago that I would never get involved with someone who does drugs. I'm sorry."

I pull his hand off my face and turn to leave once more. He clambers around me and blocks the front door. His smile is gone and I can only imagine how I must be killing his high.

"I only smoke after work and sometimes on the weekend. It's not a debilitating addiction, but I can understand why you might feel hesitant. What if I promise never to smoke around you?"

The smell of the smoke on his breath is starting to turn me off and I instantly shake my head.

"All right, come with me," he says, grabbing my hand and pulling me toward the bedroom. "Just go sit in there and I'll be right back."

I sigh as I trudge back into the bedroom and sit on the edge of the bed. The faucet turns on in the bathroom and I imagine he's probably in there brushing his teeth and gargling some minty mouthwash. He finally comes back and I can smell the mouthwash as he sits next to me without saying anything.

"Are you okay?" I ask.

He finally smiles and grabs my hand. "You wanted to know why I left Wilmington to come here." He takes a deep breath and stretches his neck before he continues. "I almost killed someone three months ago."

I want to pull my hand out of his, but now I'm afraid

of what he'll do. "What do you mean by *almost?*"

"I told you I have—*had*—problems controlling my temper. It started after I quit competing two years ago. Instead of getting depressed, I got angry."

He squeezes my hand tighter. Between this and the look Jo gave me when she offered to take my shift, I'm beginning to understand that we all must be walking around with secrets that eat away at us, driving us to do foolish things in the name of keeping those secrets buried.

"I caught my ex making out with some guy outside her apartment," he continues. "I went there to surprise her when she thought I was in class and I saw her pinned against her front door with this guy's hand in her crotch. I fucking flipped. I just kept pummeling the shit out of him. I couldn't stop. I took court-ordered anger management classes then I moved here. Some crazy idea that being closer to the water would help." He's squeezing my hand too hard now and I wriggle my fingers to loosen his grip. He brings my knuckles to his lips and kisses me as he looks up. "I can't even imagine what it must have been like to lose your mom that way."

Something about the way his eyebrows crinkle together makes me lose it. "I didn't know she was dead. Well, I didn't want to accept it. I convinced myself that she was just sleeping... for more than thirty hours. The neighbor, who my mother had led me to believe was my grandmother, came by to drop off some food and found my mom. The cops found me hiding in the nook between the refrigerator and the wall. That was where my mom always told me to hide whenever her dealer came over or when she left me home alone so she could score a fix. That was where I felt safe."

He wraps his arm around my shoulder and I slump over, burying my face in my hands. I wish I could tell him everything that's happened since that day; everything up until the day I moved into this apartment. Maybe he would understand. No, he couldn't. It's been months and even I don't understand.

"Every night, when I go to sleep, there's one memory I hold onto and relive in my mind—every single night." I look up and into his face, willing myself not to cry. "The week before she died, she invited a man over—not to have sex or anything; he was just a friend she invited over once in a while. They were sitting on the sofa talking while I was watching cartoons, pretending not to listen to their conversation, and the man said something I'll never forget. He said, "Life is only as hard as you make it, Kell. You have to let go of the past or keep carrying it on your back like a fucking pile of bricks."" I take a deep breath as I remember how seven-year-old me had smiled when he cursed. "Redneck wisdom, but I took it to heart."

"So that's why you moved here? To let go of your past?" I nod and he smiles at me. "I guess we both had to lose something to find each other."

I stare at the sweet smile on his face for a moment before my gaze falls to the tattoo on his chest. Then I glance at the glass of ice water on the nightstand and back to his face. He followed the direction of his compass to the water and it brought him to me.

I don't want to feel this way about Adam. I don't want to move on from what happened so quickly. I'm supposed to wallow in self-pity or denial for a long time. That's how these things work. This feels wrong and fast, like I'm barreling down a hill in a car with no brakes. I'm going to crash and body parts are going to fly—in particular, hearts. I can feel it.

But I don't care.

I grab handfuls of his hair and pull his face toward me, mashing his lips against mine as I climb onto his lap. His tongue searches my mouth as his arms wrap around my waist pulling me against him. I reach down to pull my dress up and he grabs my hands.

"Wait," he whispers as he rests his forehead against mine and pulls my hands together in front of his chest. "I don't want you to do this if you're not ready."

"I'm ready," I respond quickly, but he doesn't let go of my hands.

"No, you're not."

"Yes, I am."

"Claire, I'm stoned and even *I* can see that you're not ready."

He lets go of my hands and my fists fall softly against his chest. He kisses the tip of my nose and I press my lips together to hide my smile.

"This is pretty," I say as I bring my fingertip to the top of his tattoo and trace the circular compass.

He draws in a sharp breath as his skin prickles with goose bumps. "That's what I was going for. I told the tattoo artist, "Give me your prettiest tattoo," and it was either this or a pink butterfly. The butterfly's on my ass."

"I want one."

"You want a tattoo or a tattoo artist?"

I rake my fingers over his chest and up to his collarbone before I wrap my arms around neck. "Can you take me to get one?"

"I don't know. I think I've already been a bad enough influence on you."

"Please. You have this cool little mantra right over your heart. I have a mantra, too."

He cocks an eyebrow as he leans in to kiss my jaw. "What's your mantra?"

"You're not going to like it. Nobody likes it. I got it from a book on Buddhism. Not that I'm Buddhist, I just read a couple of books and this one sentence sort of stuck with me."

His lips trace a light trail down to my neck and I have to stop myself from grinding against him. "Just spit it out."

I draw in a sharp breath as his tongue slides across my

collarbone and he lays a soft kiss on my shoulder. "I am in training to be nobody special," I whisper.

He freezes for a moment then looks up at me. "What does that mean?"

"It means I'm not fighting the tide trying to be something great or memorable. I am in training to be nobody special. I go with the flow or, as you might say, I'm riding it out."

He chuckles as he shakes his head. "You're right. I hate it."

"Hey! I didn't talk trash about your mantra."

"That's because mine's awesome," he says as his fingers roam over my back.

"Ride it out? Oh, how profound."

"And aiming to be nobody special is profound? It's not profound, it's depressing. Besides, you could never be nobody special."

CHAPTER TEN

Relentless Laughter

Adam stops by the café every single day this week on his way to work, as if to prove that ignoring me all last week was just a fluke and that he's taking his *stalker gig* seriously. The best part of his visits is how much Linda and my coworkers like him. He actually convinced Linda to let him give her a lesson in how to dance "Gangnam Style" in front of six other customers. Watching Adam and my boss groovin' out in the middle of the café caused major swoonage. Despite these picture-perfect morning meetings, I have yet to see Adam after work.

"I'm telling you, he's a male stripper and he doesn't want you to see him come home covered in kiss marks and the stench of cheap perfume," Senia says, twisting open a bottle of Coke for us to drink with the pizza we ordered.

"He's not a stripper. He works for his dad's

construction company," I say as I grab a slice of cheese pizza and the glass of soda Senia just poured for me. I lean back on the sofa and take a sip before I continue. "Then again, he does seem to be a good dancer."

"You know what they say about good dancers." She wiggles her eyebrows and I try not to blush.

"I may never know if that's true."

"You should ask him to go on a double date with us," she says before taking a gigantic bite of her pizza. "We should go to that new hookah bar."

"Hey, skank. No talking with your mouthful." I take a few gulps of soda as I consider her offer.

The last time I went on a double date with Senia was when she and her freshman boyfriend, Tar Heel point guard Kevin Brown, took her, Chris, and me, to a frat party where she got so drunk she pissed in Kevin's lap. They broke up five minutes later and I'm not allowed to speak of that night.

I would love to see Adam charm the pants off Senia and Eddie, but I'm also nervous about taking him out in public with that temper of his. Especially since something tells me he still hasn't told me the whole story behind it. Somehow, I doubt that quitting surfing was the reason he developed anger issues. And if I don't know what really triggered it, I don't know if I'll be leading him into a potentially volatile situation.

"Claaaaaaire!" Senia whines, and I set down my pizza

and soda on the coffee table. "Please come with us. I promise I won't make fun of his dance moves or how he hasn't gone *Gangnam Style* on you yet."

"I don't know if a hookah bar is the best place for him," I reply, thinking of how lame he'll probably think it is to smoke flavored tobacco compared to his normal greenery.

"Why?"

I shrug and purse my lips and make a few more skeptical faces before I finally answer. "Adam's a pothead."

"Big fuckin' deal, so is Eddie. At least now we know they'll get along."

"Eddie smokes pot?"

"Yeah, I just always tell him to do it before he comes over so you don't get pissed."

"I wouldn't have gotten pissed."

"Well, I was just trying to be sensitive to… you know."

I shake my head then kiss her cheek. "I don't deserve a friend like you."

"You're damn right," she says, pushing me away. "You deserve better."

"You're right, but I'll settle for you any day."

"God damn, you know just what to say to get my panties wet."

The knock at the door startles both of us and Senia splashes Coke all over the sage-green sofa we went halves on last month.

"Shit!" she yelps as she slams her glass on the coffee table and races to the kitchen to grab some paper towels.

I haven't checked on Cora yet today, but she rarely ever knocks on our door. She doesn't like leaving Bigfoot unattended for more than a couple of minutes at a time. Maybe Adam is finally going to make an appearance. It is Thursday, after all. It's almost the weekend.

I answer the door and stare at the guy standing in front of me for far too long. He finally clears his throat and I chuckle awkwardly.

"Sorry. Can I help you?"

He holds a simple bouquet of wildflowers tied with a lavender ribbon. "Are you Claire Nixon?"

"Yes."

"Sign here."

He hands me a clipboard and I sign next to the X. He hands me the flowers then mutters something about having a good night before he jogs away toward a white van.

I shut the front door and find Senia spraying Windex on the sofa and sopping up the Coke spill with gobs of wadded-up paper towels.

"Are those from him?" she asks as she sprays more Windex on the expensive sofa.

I'm a bit dazed as I pull the card out of the bouquet and open it.

These flowers are nothing special, unlike you.

It's like the guy has radar. He can sense when he's moving up my shit list. And he knows just what to say to get back in my good graces.

"What if he has a double-life?" I say as I sit back on my side of the sofa and inhale a large whiff of the sweetly scented flowers. "Maybe he has a girlfriend back in Wilmington who he visits during the week."

"Now you're just being paranoid," she says as she gathers the used-up paper towels and heads back to the kitchen. "What does the card say?"

"These flowers are nothing special, unlike you."

"Ugh!" she groans. "You told him your mantra!"

I'm not in the mood to have my mantra crapped on again so I ignore her while I continue sniffing my flowers. They're wild and beautiful and so much classier than a dozen roses. He knows me better than I would expect.

"Maybe he *is* a stalker!" I shout back at her just as she comes out of the kitchen.

She plops down next to me and grabs the TV remote off the coffee table. "Maybe you should stop overanalyzing this."

When I text Adam to thank him for the flowers and

ask if he wants to go to a hookah bar with us Friday night, he responds with what could possibly be the hottest text message I've ever received.

Adam: *I wouldn't miss the chance to see your sexy lips wrapped around my hookah.*

AFTER SENIA INTRODUCES Adam to Eddie and they make a few dumb jokes about going to get some hookahs (pronouncing it like hook-uhs), the four of us walk to the hookah lounge from the apartment. The lounge is less than half a mile away, but Eddie cannot keep his hands off Senia the entire way there. Adam and I walk a few paces behind them, watching as Eddie's hand slides underneath the back of her T-shirt and she pushes him away when she realizes he's trying to undo her bra.

I glance sideways at Adam just as he glances at me and I smile. "You'll get used to it. Senia and Eddie are PDA Central."

"It doesn't bother me," he says as he laces his fingers through mine and brings my hand to his lips. "It's nice to see two people who aren't afraid to make their feelings known."

I'm not sure if he's implying that I'm afraid of sharing my feelings with him, but I try to follow Senia's advice and not overanalyze his words or actions. I focus instead on the beautiful beach houses and quaint shops we pass as we walk down Lumina. He squeezes my hand and I look away from the scenery to find him pointing toward a small house with blue shutters and a Jeep parked in the driveway.

"I have a meeting with the guy who lives there tomorrow, Jason Wicker. He's a surf instructor on Shell Island and he wants me to work with him on weekends. I told him my weekends belong to you, but he wouldn't take no for an answer."

"Your weekends don't belong to me," I reply quickly, ignoring the pang of disappointment at the thought of spending even less time with him. "You should work with him. You need to get back out there."

"It's not like I don't still surf. What do you think I'm doing every night when you don't see me?"

My eyes widen as I realize I've been a complete dope, cooking up all these unsavory scenarios in my head for the ways he spends his free hours. When I don't answer he shakes my hand to prompt a response.

"What did you think I was doing?"

I shrug as my ears burn with embarrassment. "Senia and I considered a few different scenarios."

"Such as?"

"Such as… a stripper."

He laughs so hard he has a coughing fit. Senia and Eddie turn around to see what the fuss is about and I wave at them to let them know everything's okay.

"You thought I was a stripper?"

"That was Senia's suggestion."

"Tell her I said thank you. What was *your* suggestion?"

"It's not important."

"Aw, come on." He steps in front of me and busts out the puppy dog eyes as he walks backward. "Please. I'll give you a free lap dance."

I push him hard in the chest and he grabs my wrist. His other arm hooks around my waist and he yanks me flush against him.

"What you think of me is *very* important," he says in a harsh whisper that frightens and thrills me all at once. He leans in closer and smiles against my lips, but he doesn't kiss me.

My heart thumps against my chest as I smile, waiting for him to kiss me because I know he's waiting for me to give in. He lets go of my wrist and his fingertips brush my jaw as he plants a soft kiss on the corner of my lips.

He pulls away and squints at me as if he's trying to figure me out. "You're going to be my downfall."

He grabs my hand and we pick up our pace to catch up with Senia and Eddie.

"I suggested that you might be a stalker," I admit, and from the corner of my eye I glimpse him shaking his head.

"You're testing my patience, Claire."

"I'm just being honest. You've known more about me

than I've known about you from the second we met. I'm sitting in my apartment wondering why the fuck I only see you on weekends while you're pumping Cora for information on me. You do realize that's not fair."

"All Cora told me about you was that you moved into the building in May and that you and I could be friends. That doesn't make me a stalker." He chuckles when he says *stalker*. "Have you ever considered that you might be a bit easier to read than you think you are?"

I shake my head as we cross the street toward the hookah lounge. "You think you have me figured out because you sent me the right kind of flowers and you guessed that I dropped out of school? Well, let me tell you something, Adam, you know the Claire Nixon that moved here three months ago. And I'm starting to think that's all you'll ever know."

When we arrive at the hookah lounge, he opens the door for us to go inside, but he refuses to look at me. We sit at a booth with a low table in front of us and Adam immediately snatches the menu off the table. Senia cocks an eyebrow at me as she begins to sense the tension between Adam and me. I scoot closer to her and farther from him, shaking my head so she doesn't mention it, and she rolls her eyes.

"Cranberry juice shisha? What a fuckin' joke," Adam says as he tosses the menu onto the table and reaches into his pocket. "I've got something that doesn't sound like a fucking drink mixer."

He tucks his hand behind his back as the waitress comes by and asks for our order and what kind of pipe we'd like to smoke out of. I don't say a word because I won't be smoking any of it. Adam orders a water pipe and points at the first flavor on the menu: Kiwi. As the waitress leaves, his eyes follow her ass for a few seconds before he turns back to us.

"Don't they have water in this place?" I ask, suddenly parched.

"We'll get you some water, babe," Senia assures me as Adam glances around the lounge as if we don't exist.

Eddie looks at Senia questioningly and she whispers something in his ear. His eyes widen a little as if he understands, but he never looks at Adam or me.

I never really had friends until Chris got me to open up. Chris was my best friend until I met Senia so it kills me to see her whispering secrets to Eddie. A small part of me is jealous that she has something to share with him that she can't share with me, but I know the whispering probably has more to do with Adam's presence than mine.

"Claire, can you please join me in the girls' room?" Senia asks sweetly.

Eddie stands up so Senia and I can slide out of the booth. I move quickly toward the restroom sign I see in the corner near the entrance, eager to get away from Adam and his shitty attitude. I should have never asked him to come out on a Friday.

As soon as we enter the restroom, Senia rounds on me. "What the fuck is up with you two?"

"I don't know. One minute we're joking about him being a stripper, the next minute he's kissing me, then the next second I'm "testing his patience". He's got multiple personalities."

Senia rolls her eyes. "Woman, he doesn't have multiple personalities. He's in love."

"What? That's stupid."

The restroom door opens and Senia shakes her head as she scoots out of the way for three girls to enter. "It's not stupid. I'm sorry, Claire, but you were spoiled by Chris. He was too patient with you because he knew that was what you needed. But the problem is now you don't know how most guys behave when they're in love."

"He's not in love. We've known each other for two weeks."

"It doesn't matter. The guy is either in love or jonesin' for your hoo-hah. Just do me a favor and trust me when I say you need, need, need to let yourself experience this. Even if it's just a fling. He's the kind of guy who can help you put that other shit behind you."

"Or bring it all to the surface and cause a mental breakdown. I haven't told you about our little bet, have I?"

"What bet?"

A girl wearing way too much eyeliner smiles at me as

she exits the restroom, as if she knows what bet I'm referring to.

Once she's gone I sigh. "He bet me that he could get me to tell him why I dropped out. If he wins, I have to go back to school."

"Whoa, whoa, whoa… You agreed to this?"

"I know. It's so stupid."

"No, it's not. It's brilliant!"

The restroom door opens again and this time it's a guy who's actually kind of hot but obviously stoned. His eyes widen when he sees us and he quickly apologizes as he closes the door.

"It's not brilliant. I've been out of school too long and you know I can't go back to Raleigh."

Just saying the name aloud makes my body tense. Everything and everybody I've ever known is in Raleigh. Every memory of my mother and Chris are there. Of course, the person I've been trying to avoid more than anyone is there: Jackie Knight. If Jackie knew what I did after Chris left, she would hate me more than she probably already does since I disappeared. She might even hate me more than I hate myself.

"You can go back, and you should, but that's a whole other two-hour argument we can rehash later." Senia grabs my arms and stares at me, her eyes pleading. "For now, just go out there and try to have some fun. Please."

I wriggle out of her grasp and shrug as I reach for the

door handle and yank it open. "I can have fun without being a fucking doormat."

I storm out of the restroom and back to our booth. When I get there, I find Adam and Eddie laughing about something as Adam passes the hookah pipe across the table. The smell of the pot is hardly noticeable through the thick cloud of sweetly scented tobacco smoke. When Adam sees me he immediately stands so I can scoot in on his side. Maybe Eddie had a talk with him, as well.

He smiles as I slide in. He sits down and immediately leans over to whisper in my ear. "You look beautiful tonight. I forgot to tell you that earlier."

I can smell the smoke on his breath, but the sensation of his lips against my ear is enough to almost make me forget why I was mad at him. I turn my face toward him so our noses are touching and his gaze slides down to my lips.

"I don't think you're a stalker," I whisper. "I think… I wish you were around more often."

It makes my chest ache with anxiety just to say these words aloud. I don't want to open myself up to him like this, but Senia is right. I need this, whether it's a fling or something more. I don't want to end up a brittle old broad or, worse, a terrified shut-in like my mom.

He smiles before he plants a soft kiss on my lips and I put my hand on top of his thigh to steady myself. He pulls away and kisses my forehead. "I'll take you out with me next time I go to the beach."

I nod, too afraid that if I speak something even cornier may come out. I glance at Senia next to me and she's pretending not to notice this exchange between Adam and me. One thing I can say about Senia is that she is great at being discreet when it's necessary.

Senia and I refuse to smoke both the tobacco and the weed, but I soon start to feel as if my brain is becoming as foggy as this room. Adam's laughter begins to sound a bit distant, like canned laughter in a sitcom. I blink furiously, as if this will wake me up, and Adam looks at me funny.

"Are you okay?" he asks.

"I feel like I'm in a movie. You look like a movie star." I reach out and touch his face. "You have facial hair and it feels so scratchy. I'm thirsty." I reach for the glass of water in front of me, but it's empty. "I'm so thirsty."

"Aw, shit. You have a contact high. I think it's time to get you home." He stands up and nods toward the exit. "Come on. You need some fresh air."

Senia and Eddie stay behind while Adam walks me home. The cool night air feels like heaven on my skin, but the sidewalk looks like a treadmill belt. I'm getting nowhere. By the time I arrive at my apartment, I'm feeling more clearheaded, though I have no memory of how we got there.

"Is Eddie staying over?" Adam asks as I dig inside my purse for my keys.

I laugh way harder at this than I should. "You want me

to spend the night again."

He shakes his head. "Just trying to save you from having to listen to Senia and Eddie doing all the things we should be doing."

"I can't see anything in this purse. It's too dark." Finally, I shove my purse into his chest and he grins. "All right, Adam, you want to have sex with me? You think you can handle this?" I giggle uncontrollably because I know I'm being ridiculous, but I can't stop. "Bring it."

He grabs my hand and pulls me toward the stairs. "Oh, it's already been broughten."

I laugh as I climb the stairs behind him. "I love that you always get my movie references. You're so funny… and hot."

He chuckles as he climbs the last few stairs and reaches into his pocket for his keys. "I need to get you stoned more often."

CHAPTER ELEVEN

Relentless Guilt

I OPEN MY eyes and stare at the oscillating fan next to the bed. Even with the fan pointed straight at me, I'm still sweating and I quickly understand why. Adam's chest is pressed against my back and I'm wearing nothing but a bra and panties. I have a vague memory of tearing off my tank top and shorts, but I can't remember much else.

His arm is wrapped around my waist and his breath is hot against the back of my head. Our bodies are sticky everywhere our skin is touching. It's unbearably hot and humid in here. On the bright side, he's not suffering from morning wood syndrome.

I need to get out of here. I have a bad feeling we had forgettable sex and I don't want to admit that I can't remember it. I slowly attempt to scoot forward to peel my back off his chest and he grunts as he tightens his arm around my waist.

"Go back to sleep," he groans, and now that I know he's awake I let out the breath I've been holding.

"What time is it? I work at three."

"It's still morning. Go back to sleep."

"I can't. It's too hot in here."

"Then take these off," he says, hooking his thumb into the waistband of my panties. "I'd be happy to help you with that."

I roll over to face him and he whips his head out of the way so I don't elbow him in the face.

"Hey, Smokey the Bear," I say. God, he looks so sexy when he's groggy. "You think you're so hot, but I don't even remember what happened last night so it can't be that good."

He laughs in my face and I can still smell a hint of smoke on his breath. "That's because nothing happened last night."

"Nothing happened?"

"You walked into my room, stripped down to your underwear, made some comment about this being the most comfortable bed in the universe, and knocked out."

"Oh... Somehow, I find that a little disappointing."

"You're bummed we didn't have forgettable sex? Or you're bummed we didn't have sex?"

The truth is, I'm a little disappointed we haven't gotten the whole *first time* thing out of the way. It's too much pressure. I haven't been with anyone other than Chris and, like Senia said last night, he spoiled me. He waited more than two years before we had sex on my eighteenth birthday. I've only known Adam two weeks, but this need to get the sex over with tells me that we should probably wait.

"I guess I'm disappointed we didn't have sex," I reply, because I know that's what he wants to hear.

"You *guess* you're disappointed?" He brushes a lock of hair away from my face and lifts my chin so he can look me in the eye. "You're not a virgin, are you?"

"What? No!" I don't know why I'm so adamant with my response. "I am *not* a virgin." *Though part of me wishes I were.*

He smiles as he slips his arm around my waist and pulls me closer. I swallow hard as his erection jabs my thigh through his boxers.

Oh, God.

He leans in to kiss me and, as soon as his lips touch mine, my body relaxes into him. I slide my arms around his neck as he rolls me onto my back. He pushes my legs open with his knee as his fingers skates up my side. His tongue flirts with mine and my nipples perk up beneath the fabric of my bra. He grinds against me as his hand cups my breast and I know this is it. We're going to have sex.

He slips his hand underneath me and pulls his head back when his fingers find the hook on my bra. "Is this okay?" he asks.

My heart is pounding, but the need throbbing between my legs is more intense.

"I want this," I say with a nod. "I want you."

He unhooks my bra and watches as I slide the straps down. I toss it over the edge of the bed and he gazes at me with a deep sense of wonderment and longing in his eyes. He lays a soft trail of kisses from my sternum to my breast and I let out a small gasp as he takes my nipple into his mouth.

His fingers move lightly over my belly to my hip. He grasps the waist of my panties and looks up at me, his eyes questioning if he can remove these, too. I nod and lift my hips so he can slip them off. He takes off his boxers and he supports his weight on his elbows as he kisses me slowly. His lips graze my jaw as he moves to my neck then down to my breast again. He keeps going until his head is between my legs.

He looks up at me, a smile in his eyes, then his mouth is on me. His tongue swirls around my swollen clit and, it's been so long, it doesn't take much. I come quick and probably too loudly. His body slides over mine as he slinks up and kisses my forehead. He smiles as he slips a condom out of his nightstand and rips it open with his teeth.

I can't breathe.

The nurse wheels me out of the hospital room and, after what

I've just been through, I'm surprised I have enough energy to be frightened by the sight of the person standing ten feet ahead of me next to the nurses' station. Joanie Tipton hands the nurse behind the desk a piece of paper then turns toward me.

Senia steps in front of the wheelchair to block me from Joanie's view, but it's too late. Joanie has already seen me. And by the shit-eating grin on her face, she knows exactly why I'm here.

Of all the people in the world, Joanie is the last person I want to see here. She's had it out for me since our senior year in high school when Chris and I were broken up for three weeks and he still rejected her invitation to the prom. She showed up at the Knights' house the day before he left in July to wish him well. Chris and I were just getting ready to leave to celebrate my birthday a month early. Later that night, I used Joanie as an example of all the groupies Chris would have access to on tour. I told him we should break up so he could get all that stuff out of his system. I didn't think I could handle finding out he'd faltered while we were still together.

Joanie doesn't know I used her crush on Chris as an example of why we should break up, but as she stands there smiling at me I know she will move mountains to tell him she saw me here today.

I'm not in the right state of mind to deal with Joanie. My chest muscles ache from three days of uncontrollable sobbing and I'm woozy from the mild sedative I was given twenty minutes ago. As she approaches us on her way down the corridor, the panic builds inside me, but it manifests only in tears.

"What the fuck are you staring at?" Senia snarls at her, and Joanie's smile vanishes just as she disappears somewhere behind the *wheelchair.*

The nurse continues to push my wheelchair forward, but everything moves in slow motion compared to my racing heartbeat. She's going to tell Chris everything and this time I'll lose him forever.

"Claire."

Adam's voice shakes the memory loose and I open my eyes to find him sitting next to me instead of lying on top of me. Cool tears stream down my temples and into my hair. I quickly wipe them away before I sit up and curl my legs into my chest.

"What happened?" I ask as I stare at the foot of the bed to avoid looking at him.

I don't want to see the expression on his face. I don't want to see just how crazy he thinks I am.

"Nothing. You squeezed your eyes shut and started crying. Nothing happened. I swear."

I feel exposed, emotionally and physically. I want to gather my clothes and get out of here, but I'm too afraid to move.

"Do you want to tell me what happened?"

I shake my head as I straighten my legs out in front of me and pull the sheet up to my chest to cover myself. "You think you want to know what happened—what made me drop out—but you don't understand that if I tell you you'll want nothing more to do with me."

"You don't know that."

He brushes my messy hair out of my eyes and the look in his eyes breaks my heart. I will never tell him.

"Come here," he whispers as he pulls me into his arms.

As soon as I press the side of my face to his shoulder, the tears come again. What the hell was I thinking? Enough time hasn't passed since that day in the hospital. I should have known it was too soon.

CHAPTER TWELVE

Relentless Waves

AFTER SATURDAY'S BREAKDOWN, I'm shocked that he still wants me to go to the beach with him on Wednesday night, my only day off from the café this week. I spend all day Wednesday at the apartment. I immediately get caught up in an endless loop of watching recorded episodes of *Vampire Diaries*, doing laundry, and meditating. By the time Senia gets home early from work, I've washed all our clothes and linens and meditated four times. I haven't felt this relaxed in weeks.

She hangs her purse up on the peg inside the coat closet and plops down next to me on the sofa. "I can't work with him anymore!"

I know she's referring to her dad. He spoils her financially, but he's also extremely controlling. Growing up, her father dictated what Senia and her two sisters wore, ate, and who they befriended up until they graduated from high school. She wasn't allowed to date until her senior year and only then because her date was a friend of the family. When she got to UNC two years ago, she was a completely different person than she is now. She was scared and shy, but it didn't take long for the real Senia to emerge. In the beginning of our freshman year, it was the alcohol that brought her out. Eventually she stopped getting drunk every weekend.

The first time she talked back to her father was when he refused to put the pink slip for her car in her name. She knew he only wanted the car in his name so he could use the car as a means to control her. From the moment she told him to *fuck off* their relationship changed. He now only speaks to her when he needs to for work purposes. Their relationship is almost enough to make me grateful I never knew my father.

"What did he do today?" I ask as I reach for the remote.

"Why do you ask like that, like you're tired of hearing me complain about my job?"

"I'm sorry. I didn't mean to give off that vibe. I guess it was just a bad word choice. I should have left off "today"."

Senia sighs as she puts her feet up on the coffee table. "It's okay. I'm just really annoyed right now. He wants me to move back in this weekend. I told him there's still four more weeks before the semester starts, but he said he would take my car away if I don't go back to working at the main office, where he can keep an eye on me. He's tired of me leaving work early."

"And your response was to leave work early?"

She turns to me and I can see by the apologetic look in her eyes that she agreed to her father's demands. "I'm so sorry, Claire, but I need my car."

I nod and manage a weak smile. "It's no big deal. I can find another roommate. And, hey, Linda might actually give me more hours if I ask Adam to go on a date with her."

"God, I feel like such a dirt-bag leaving you hanging like this. I really wanted to spend the rest of the summer here."

"Don't feel bad," I say, grabbing her hand. "I'll be fine. And you and Eddie are welcome to hang out or sleepover whenever you want."

She stares at me for a moment and I can see the wheels turning in her head. "You should move in with—"

"Don't say it!"

"Whatever. Are you two still going surfing today?"

"Yeah, unless you want to do something. I feel like I should be spending the rest of this week with you."

"Oh, please. You act like I'm dying in four days."

"Well, not *all* of you."

"Yeah, just the part that loves watching you meditate."

At exactly six in the evening, a knock comes at the

door. I'm ready with my yellow bikini underneath my faded-blue Roxy T-shirt and a pair of white board shorts that I usually only wear around the house because they barely cover my ass, but Senia insisted I wear them. I'm excited. I've seen guys—hot guys—surfing at the beach dozens of times since I moved to Wrightsville Beach, but something about getting to see Adam out there gives me butterflies. I'm finally going to get to share his passion for the water with him. And enough time, and meditation, has passed between Saturday and today that I'm feeling a lot less guilty about leaving him hanging.

I open the door and Adam is leaning against the doorframe with one hand in the pocket of his board shorts. He's shirtless so even when he looks up at me with those striking green eyes, all I can look at is his perfectly muscular chest.

"Are you ready to get tossed?"

"Is that a promise?" I say as I step outside.

He laughs as he throws his arms around my waist, lifts me off the ground, and kisses me. His lips are warm and soft as I take his bottom lip between my teeth.

He moans softly and I feel him stiffening against me. "You'd better stop that or I'm going to take you upstairs right now."

I give him a soft peck on the lips then tighten my arms around his neck as I lay my head on his shoulder. He squeezes me tightly and I sigh. This is the best hug I've gotten in months. He finally sets me down and cradles my face as he kisses both my eyelids.

"Thanks for coming with me."

I grin uncontrollably because something has shifted between us. Something magical is happening. I feel deliriously happy for the first time since Chris left.

Adam says he normally walks to the beach, but today we're taking the truck because he brought an extra surfboard for me. He parks in front of a house near the beach and carries both our boards across the sand. He lays the boards flat on the damp sand near the edge of the water and looks at me.

"Have you ever surfed?"

"I have, actually. Fallon, the girl who taught me to meditate, tried to teach me a couple of times. I actually stood up on the board once."

"Good," he says, tucking his board under his arm. "Then I don't have to go through all the standard stuff about how to pop up."

"Really? We're just going to go right out?"

"Claire, the sun's going down in less than two hours. You won't be able to surf after the sun goes down."

"But you do."

"Because I don't need to see the water to know where it's going."

I can't help but sigh as I peel off my clothes. "That is so hot."

"Besides, the sharks come out at night."

"Sharks!"

He shakes his head as he bounds toward the water. I grab my board and follow after him. Once we're waist deep in the warm Atlantic Ocean, we're forced to continually duck dive under the relentless waves until we're far enough past the breaks. We paddle out a bit further until we get to a place where we can turn around to face the beach. I can hardly breathe and my limbs ache. My arms tremble as I climb onto the board to straddle it the way Adam does.

"Are you okay?"

I nod because I don't have enough air in my lungs to speak.

The rolling motion of the water is carrying our boards farther apart and making me a little queasy. He holds his hand out to me. I take his hand and he yanks me toward him.

"Okay, I'm going to tell you something I never tell anybody when they ask me for a surfing lesson."

"What?"

"You look really sexy in that bikini."

"And you'd better not tell anyone else that."

"Ooh, you wear jealousy even better than you wear that bikini," he says as he leans over and kisses my temple. "You should take it off."

"Focus, Adam."

"Right." He gazes at the waves as they crash onto the

shore before us for a while before he speaks again. What he says has nothing to do with surfing. "I want you to meet my parents."

"That's your idea of focusing?"

He tilts his head as he looks at me because he knows I'm trying to avoid the subject.

"You don't have to, but I'm going there this weekend. They're having their annual summer picnic on my uncle's ranch and I want you to come with me because I don't think I can handle being away from you all weekend."

I recognize that jittery feeling in my belly, and it's the feeling that scares me more than what Adam's proposing. I can feel myself falling. Hard. If I meet his parents, it will be like completely giving into that feeling. This won't be infatuation anymore. It will be serious.

Say something, Claire, my inner voice shouts at me.

"Okay."

"You'll go?"

I nod fiercely and he leans over to kiss me so fast we both flip our boards and slip into the water. A tangle of seaweed snags on my foot and I scream. He laughs as he gathers our boards.

"All right, no more fooling around. I'm about to give you a serious lesson." We climb back onto our boards and hold hands as we watch the waves break against the shore. "Pay attention to the rhythm and movement of the water."

He lets go of my hand and I draw in a deep breath.

The water dips and surges beneath my board and I can feel my body relaxing as I grip the rails, paying close attention. There's a definite rhythm to the rise and crash of each wave. Without knowing, I realize I've closed my eyes and I'm visualizing the waves based on the sound. It's so peaceful out here.

"Are you ready?" he asks, and I nod as I open my eyes.

He points at the waves as he tells me what to do. I try to repeat all his instructions in my head as I lie down on the board. *Push the nose down… lean into the direction of the wave… Let the momentum of the water carry you.*

He shoves my board forward and shouts, "Start paddling!"

My first lesson is a disaster so as soon as the sun starts to set behind us, I breathe a sigh of relief and make my way back to solid ground. My jelly legs give out beneath me and I fall to my knees next to my beach bag. I wipe the saltwater from my face with a towel, lay the towel out on the sand, and collapse facedown.

"Hey, you didn't do too bad," Adam says as he pulls a bottle of water out of my beach bag and hands it to me.

I take the water and turn onto my side so I can guzzle it down. "Yeah, not so bad. I never once stood up."

"That's okay for your first time out. In fact, it's expected. Trust me, I'll have you riding in the curl soon."

"Are you going to take that weekend job on Shell Island?"

"Are you going to be my first student?"

"I can't afford surf lessons."

"I'm sure Jason won't mind me donating some lessons to a few hopeless cases every now and then."

I roll my eyes as I turn over onto my back. "I don't have the energy to be outraged by that comment."

We're both silent for a moment before I realize that the sun is about to set. I sit up and the intense look in his eyes tells me his mind is far away from this beach right now. He grabs my hand and the sand rubs between our wrinkled palms as he laces his fingers through mine.

"Claire, I asked you to go with me this weekend for more than one reason." He pauses for a moment before he peels his gaze away from the dazzling pink sunset to look at me. "I'm falling in love with you." I open my mouth to respond and he presses his finger against my lips to stop me. "I don't want you to say anything. I just want you to know that. I love you."

He waits a moment before he removes his finger from my lips.

I want to say it back because I think he deserves to hear it and because I do feel something strong like love growing inside of me. But I'm not certain yet. I scoot forward a little on my towel so our sides are touching and lean my head on his shoulder. He kisses my forehead as he wraps his towel around me. We watch the sunset in silence as I think to myself, *Adam loves the sunset* and *me*.

CHAPTER THIRTEEN

Relentless Bickering

"ARE YOU SURE you don't need any more help packing?" I ask as I slip my feet into some strappy wedge sandals.

"If you ask me that one more time I'm going to hide your keys and lock you out of this apartment," Senia says, pushing me out of the bedroom. "Get out of here. Go ride some horses on your cowboy's ranch. And while you're at it, ride your cowboy."

"It's not his ranch."

"Don't sass me, Claire; just do as you're told."

She pushes me all the way to the front door, still managing to grab my purse off the breakfast bar along the way. She pushes the purse into my chest and I pull her into a bone-crushing hug.

"I'm going to miss having you here," I blubber into her hair. "Who am I going to watch Toni Collette movies with on my birthday?"

"Girl, I'm taking August ninth off whether my dad likes it or not. We will be dancing and sobbing to *Muriel's Wedding* together. Now go."

I give her one last squeeze before I release her. I bite my lip as I scurry out of the apartment, trying really hard to convince myself that being separated by a hundred miles is not going to change our friendship. When I moved out of Senia's house in May, I did it knowing she had promised to spend the summer with me. Now that she's leaving four weeks early, I have to fight the sinking feeling that our friendship is going to wither like the flowers on my nightstand.

I climb the stairs to Adam's apartment and knock softly. I'm beyond nervous about meeting his family, but the thought of spending an entire weekend with them is enough to make me want to confess my secret to Adam and go back to school—anything to get out of it. I've never done well meeting new people, especially when I feel like they're scrutinizing me.

I knock again, a little harder this time, and he answers the door quickly. He's dressed, but his hair is still damp and sticking out in every direction. And he smells heavenly.

"Hey, babydoll," he says, planting a quick kiss on my lips. "Go ahead and sit down. I'm almost done."

Babydoll.

I try not to grin too widely as I head for the sofa while

he walks back to the bathroom. I can hear a blow-dryer whining as I gaze around the living room, taking in the various objects I'd never really paid too much attention to with Adam providing such a delicious distraction. In the corner, on top of his drafting table, I glimpse blueprints for some kind of building and my curiosity gets the best of me. I want to know what he spends his time looking at all those long hours we're apart.

I creep across the carpet to the desk and push the stool aside so I can get a better look at the prints. It looks like plans for a house, though I can't understand why he would have these. He told me his father's construction company only builds government buildings like prisons and military facilities.

I pull up the corner of the first page to see what's underneath when Adam's voice startles me.

"What are you doing?"

My heart hammers against my chest as I turn away from the drafting table and find him standing right next to me. "I was just looking."

His nostrils are flaring and I have a horrible feeling I've violated some sort of privacy rule I wasn't aware of.

"That's a project I've been working on for a few years. It's not finished yet."

"What is it?"

"I don't want to talk about it. Let's go."

The first ten minutes of the drive to his uncle's ranch

are filled with awkward silence followed by another ten minutes of bad pop music once he puts on the radio. When a Chris Knight song comes on, I quickly turn down the volume and pull my iPhone out of my purse. He changes lanes on the highway then turns to me, his expression still solemn.

"I'm sorry if you think I'm being unnecessarily mysterious about those house plans. I know you weren't snooping around. They're right out there where everyone can see them. But I'm not ready to talk about it yet."

"Does it have to do with why you're still working for your dad even though you detest it?"

"Sort of, yeah."

I hold up my phone and nod at the stereo. "Can you plug this in?"

He reaches across the console and takes the iPhone from my hand. It takes him a minute to plug it into his stereo as he's driving. He opens my music app and begins scrolling through the list of songs.

"You should let me do that. You're driving."

I reach for the phone, but he switches it to his left hand so I can't reach it. "Don't worry about that. I'm paying attention."

He scrolls for another minute or so until he settles on a song. The first notes play as he hands the phone back to me.

"'Waiting in Vain'?" I say. "Really? Could you be any

more of a cliché? You surf, you smoke weed, *and* you listen to Bob Marley."

"Just shut up and listen to the song. This is my song for you."

I listen to the lyrics carefully, though I already know them by heart. Bob Marley songs always remind me of the spontaneous acoustic concert Chris put on for me and a few of our friends in his parents' garage. He performed an entire set of Bob Marley songs and, though he never dedicated this song to me, it was one of his favorites.

I gaze out at the green hills along highway 74, afraid that if I look at Adam he'll see my traitorous thoughts. When the song ends, I feel like I'm expected to comment on it, but I don't know what to say. Music was something I shared with Chris. It was such a huge part of our relationship that I had to delete half my music collection after we broke up because it was driving me insane.

Adam grabs my hand and I finally turn to him. "I know you've got a lot on your mind and meeting my parents right now probably isn't at the top of your bucket list, but I want you to know that you can talk to me about it—any of it. Even if you think that what you have to say will make me uncomfortable. I'm here for you. Okay?"

I nod and give his hand a reassuring squeeze then go back to gazing out the window. There are some things that can't be discussed with a new boyfriend, like the songs that remind you of your ex. There are other things that can't be discussed with anyone.

Three hours later, we arrive at Adam's Uncle Harvey's ninety-one-acre ranch near the outskirts of Charlotte. I count eleven cars and trucks parked in a dirt lot outside a pale-yellow, two-story house with a gorgeous wrap-around porch. As soon as Adam parks his truck, two children, a boy and a girl, who look about eight or nine years old come running outside to greet him.

The girl throws her arms around Adam's neck and he laughs as he spins her around. It's a picture-perfect Hallmark moment and I feel a little like I'm intruding, so I stay on the passenger side of the truck and wait for them to finish their greetings. The boy hugs Adam around the waist and I can see the adoration in his face as he closes his eyes and buries his cheek in Adam's stomach.

"Hey, I have someone I want you to meet," Adam says, peering over his shoulder and beckoning me to his side. "Claire, this is Beatrice and Nick. They're my favorite cousins because they always let me win at Monopoly."

"We don't let you win. You cheat!" Beatrice squeals as she punches him in the arm.

Adam tickles her and all is forgiven. "Hey, don't be rude. Say hi to Claire."

"Is she your girlfriend?" Nick asks.

"She's all mine so don't get any ideas."

A man in a T-shirt, jeans, and cowboy hat comes down the front steps and I know this is Adam's father. He's very handsome for an older man, but it's the confident smile on his face that gives him away. However, he's not smiling at Adam. He's smiling at me.

"Hello there, Claire. I'm Jim Parker," he says as he approaches me. I hold out my hand and he pulls me into a tight hug. He holds on a bit longer than I expect. When he finally lets go, he looks me up and down. "No informal handshakes here. Adam told us all about you. Any girl he's willing to subject to this crowd is as good as family, as far as I'm concerned."

"Hello, Mr. Parker. It's a pleasure to meet you."

He's charming and I'm beginning to think this weekend isn't going to be so bad, until I see the look on Adam's face. His father throws him a curt nod then makes his way back to the house.

"What was that?" I whisper as Adam retrieves the small suitcase packed with our things from the cab of the truck.

He shakes his head as he slams the truck door, visibly irritated. "Trust me, you don't want to know what that was."

I follow him inside where we're bombarded with greetings from at least thirty of his family members, but none of them are his mother.

"My mom's the CFO of Parker Construction. She's even more of a workaholic than my dad," Adam whispers in my ear when I ask where she is. "He's only here early because he got in yesterday to discuss a new project with Uncle Harvey. You'll meet her in the morning."

Finally, after two hours of hearing stories about Adam's surfing achievements, which seems to make him very uncomfortable, we wrestle our way through the commotion and make it upstairs to the room we'll be staying in. As soon as he flips the light switch in the room, it's obvious we'll be staying in the bedroom of a teenage girl. Pictures of her and her friends are plastered all over the mirror and the walls. The bright-pink and black color of the striped wallpaper is echoed in the bedding. I breathe a sigh of relief that we'll at least have a full-sized bed to share.

"Whose room is this?" I ask as I reach for the zipper on the suitcase on the bed.

"My cousin Jamie. She's a freshman at UNC. She won't be here until tomorrow." He pulls my hand off the suitcase and turns me so I'm facing him. "Listen. There's a lot of bad shit between my dad and me, but that's between us. I can tell he likes you so don't let my issues with him cloud your judgment. Okay?"

"Adam, I think I'm perfectly capable of making up my own mind about your father. I mean, he seems nice enough, but I care about you. And whatever issues you have with your dad may be your business, but I want you to know that I'll always be on your side. So if you want me to be friendly with your dad, I will. But if you want me to tell him to stick his cowboy hat up his ass, I'll do that too."

"God, I fucking love you." He gives me a quick kiss before he grabs my hand. "Come on. You can unpack later. You wore your bikini under your clothes like I asked, didn't you?"

"Yeah, why?"

"We're going for a night swim in the creek."

Adam and I make our way out to the creek that runs along the west end of the property. Beatrice and Nick stay behind because they're too young, but we're joined by three of Adam's older cousins. Julia and Locke are twenty-three and fraternal twins who look nothing alike. Julia is the only one in the family with red hair and fair skin. Everyone else has the same sandy-brown hair and skin that looks like it's been crisped by long hours spent working on the ranch or surfing in the Carolina sunshine.

Julia and Locke are extremely friendly, but River is my favorite of the three. He's twenty-two, just a few months older than Adam, and the shyest of the bunch. Somehow, this puts me at ease. Everyone else exudes the same gregarious confidence as Adam. I find it comforting to know that not everyone in the Parker family is inhumanly beautiful and charismatic.

We spend almost an hour in what appears to be a muddy creek with water that reaches just to the bottom of my chin. Adam assures me it's just the lack of sunlight that makes it look murky, but I'm not convinced. Every time something brushes up against my leg, I scream and threaten to leave.

"Come on, Claire, the critters are half the fun!" Locke shouts as he hangs from a tree branch above the creek. "They're harmless so long as they don't slither into your swimsuit."

Adam grabs my foot to stop me from swimming away. "You can't leave yet." He yanks me back and wraps his arms around my waist as he pulls my back against his chest. "We haven't even played Marco Polo yet."

His hand slides over my belly and I turn around to face him. I throw my arms around his neck and wrap my legs around his waist, confident that no one can see our bodies through the black, mucky water. The startled smile on his face makes my stomach flutter. I'm pleased to see I've surprised him.

"If you take me inside," I whisper in his ear, "I'll play Marco Polo with you upstairs."

His hands slide under the waistband of my bikini and over my ass as he lets out a soft groan. He kisses my neck before he pulls his head back and looks me in the eye.

"Not here. I want our first time to be perfect and this is not the right place or the right time. Not that I don't want to take you upstairs and destroy you. Just not tonight."

"I can see your boner from here!" Julia shouts at Adam.

He shakes his head as he puts me back down on the creek bed and something definitely slithers over my foot. I kick my foot hard and end up kicking a large stone.

"Ouch!" I cry.

I can feel I've cracked my toenail and the searing pain is enough to make my eyes water.

"What happened?"

"I kicked a rock. Fuck!"

I swim quickly toward the edge of the creek and scramble out of the water. I plop down on the damp grass and try to look at my toe under the dim moonlight. It's too dark out here and my foot is covered in too much mud and grass to see whether I'm bleeding. Adam scrambles up the incline and scoops me up into his arms.

"Let's go clean it up."

"Put me down. I can walk."

"Fine."

As soon as my foot touches the ground, a sharp pain slices through my toe and I hold in my scream, but I can't hold back my grimace. I may have broken it. He reaches for me to pick me up again and I push him away.

"You're not carrying me. The house is like a quarter mile away. It's too far. I can walk."

He turns his back to me and looks over his shoulder. "Hop on my back. I'll be your horsey."

"In case you couldn't tell, I'm trying not to make several comments about riding you," I say as I climb onto his back.

"In case you couldn't tell, I'm trying really hard not to

ride you," he replies.

I try to keep my grip on his neck a bit loose so I don't choke him as he carries me all the way to the house and into the downstairs bathroom. He sets me down on the countertop and kneels down to look at my foot.

"You're too dirty," he mutters.

"That's what he said."

He shakes his head at my bad joke as he lets go of my foot. "Take a shower then I'll wrap it up for you."

"All my stuff is upstairs."

"Stay right here. I'll be right back."

A few minutes later he returns with my makeup bag and some fresh pajamas and panties.

He sets them on the countertop and stares at me for a moment before he turns to leave. "I'll be right outside. Just holler if you need anything."

He's about to shut the door when I call out to him. "Wait!"

He pops his head in and raises his eyebrows questioningly. "Did I forget something?"

"Can you stay in here with me? In case I need some help. I don't have Life Alert."

One side of his mouth pulls up in a devilish half-smile. "Of course."

He turns on the water as I untie my bikini top and climb out of my bottoms, all the while hopping on one foot and balancing my weight on the countertop. He opens the shower door and wraps his arm around my waist to help me into the shower. I pretend not to notice him staring at my breasts as I step inside and close the door behind me. The bottom of the shower turns a murky brown as the mud rinses away under the warm water.

Once the muck is gone, I can see that half my toenail is missing, but I don't think the toe is broken as it's only slightly swollen and pink.

"You okay in there?"

"I think I'm going to make it."

He opens the shower door and makes no attempt to disguise the way his eyes roam over every inch of my body. "Hey, beautiful. I'm going upstairs to use the shower up there. You sure you're okay? You don't need a hand in here?"

I throw him a thumbs-up and he smiles as he closes the door.

When I get upstairs, he's already showered and lying in the pink bed with a roll of gauze and medical tape next to him and his feet hanging off the end.

"Jamie's bed is not the most comfortable bed in the universe," he says as I set my soggy bikini down on top of the suitcase on the floor and climb into bed. "But it just got much cozier."

I hand him the gauze and the medical tape and he wraps up my toe. He kisses it softly before I tuck myself in under the covers. I switch off the lamp on the bedside table and turn onto my side. He slides in behind me to spoon me.

"You're my hero."

"I know what I'm getting you for your twenty-first birthday," he whispers in my ear as his fingertips slip under my shirt and glide over my ribcage. "Besides Life Alert."

"What are you getting me?" I ask as I try to ignore the growing gift prodding my backside.

"You'll see." He plants a soft kiss on the back of my neck then pulls my shirt down over my belly. "Goodnight, babydoll."

"Goodnight."

BREAKFAST WITH THE Parker family is a huge event and I finally get to meet his mother, Margaret Parker. She has Adam's green eyes and graceful stature combined with a gracious Southern charm. As soon as Adam and I come down for breakfast, she greets me with a warm hug and a kiss on the cheek.

"Aren't you just the prettiest thing? Look at her, Kimmy," she says to Uncle Harvey's wife, Aunt Kim, who's scooping scrambled eggs onto a long row of breakfast plates lined up on the kitchen island. "Doesn't she remind you of Winona?"

"Good morning, Mrs. Parker," I mutter, not certain if I should be flattered that I look like Winona.

Adam grabs two plates of scrambled eggs and thick-cut bacon as he squints at me. "She does kind of look like Winona with lighter hair. I never noticed it until now."

"Who's Winona?" I finally ask, taking the plate Adam hands me as we make our way to a long breakfast table stocked with a basket of blueberry muffins and a heaping plate of homemade waffles.

I grab a muffin as Margaret sits next to me. "Winona is my little sister. Or, she *was*. She died 'bout twenty years ago. You would have loved her. She was such a free spirit, like you. That must have taken a lot of courage to move all the way from Raleigh to Wrightsville all on your own."

I turn to Adam and he smiles as he keeps his eyes on his plate. "I don't know. I'm pretty used to moving around a lot. My mother died when I was seven so I moved from one foster home to another for a very long time."

Her eyebrows knit together as she rubs my back. "I'm so sorry to hear that, but happy to see that you've turned into such an independent and beautiful young woman. Some of us have more fight in us than others. Just like my Adam. You two make a fine pair."

This woman is not subtle. Between her and her husband, I'm beginning to understand why Adam was so persistent when we first met. I eat my breakfast in silence and I'm glad to help when it's time to start making potato salad, deviled eggs, and various other dishes while the men take their racks of ribs and slabs of meat out to the barbecue.

"Are you gonna be okay in here?" Adam asks as I chop celery for Aunt Kim.

"I'm fine. You go ahead and do your man stuff."

"She's fine," Margaret says as she wraps her arm around my shoulder and gives my arm a squeeze. "You go check on your father. Make sure he's not burning off what little hair he's got left."

Adam looks visibly tense at the mention of his father, but he manages to give me a quick kiss on the cheek before he scurries outside to join the men.

"A bit smaller than that, honey," Aunt Kim says while passing me on the way to the refrigerator.

Margaret watches the door for a moment after Adam leaves then turns to me. "I know this may not be any of my business, but I want you to know that Adam is crazy about you."

I smile as I grab another stalk of celery and set about chopping this one a bit smaller.

"I'm sure you've noticed the tension between him and his father."

I look sideways at her and her face is kind and inquisitive. She's not fishing for information; she's hoping to impart some wisdom.

"Yes, I've noticed that."

She breathes deeply and exhales a long breath; a breath that is probably filled with years of frustration and regret.

"Can you promise me something, honey? Because I know he can be as stubborn as a mule on Wednesday when it comes to talking about his father and you seem like the kind of girl who can get him to open up. But I need you to promise me you'll keep an open mind when he opens his heart?"

I smile even though I feel uncomfortable with her request. I don't know what she means by "when he opens his heart." What kind of secret is Adam hiding?

Margaret and I finish up the potato salad and the coleslaw. As soon as I start piping the filling into the deviled eggs, the door bursts open and Adam flies past us toward the living room. The rage rolls off him in thunderous waves as he storms out of the kitchen.

I turn to Margaret and she quickly unties the strings on the back of my apron. "Go ahead, honey. I'll finish this up."

I pull the apron over my head and hand it to her then set off through the swinging door into the living room. I glimpse Adam's feet racing up the stairs and I follow quickly behind him. When I reach Jamie's bedroom, I find him sitting on the edge of the bed with his elbows resting on the tops of his thighs and his hands clutching his hair. He's tapping his foot impatiently and I feel as if I'm edging closer to a ticking time bomb.

I step inside and close the bedroom door behind me. "Adam, are you okay?"

He shakes his head almost imperceptibly, but he

doesn't answer.

I slowly make my way across the fluffy white rug and take a seat next to him. "I know you probably think I won't understand because I never knew my father—I hardly knew my mother—but I have a lot of regrets, and pain, eating away at me over the separation from my last foster mother. I have a lot of things I want to say to her, but sometimes I think I could live my whole life without saying those things. And sometimes I think the secrets will kill me."

He lifts his head and looks at me. "My dad wants me to go to Hawaii to schmooze some government officials for a new project on the naval base."

"What's wrong with that? Hawaii is beautiful."

"If we get the project, I'll have to stay there for up to two months to handle the startup."

"Oh." I stare at the rug on the floor because I don't want him to see the disappointment in my eyes any more than he can see it in the slump of my shoulders.

"I've been trying to quit for years, but my dad won't let me." He gently turns my face toward him and the anguish in his eyes makes my chest ache. "Claire, there's something you need to know about me."

I draw in a slow breath, wishing I were at home so I could meditate. Wishing I were anywhere but here where I am about to hear a secret that may tear us apart. His mother's words repeat in my mind: *Try to keep an open mind when he opens his heart.*

"When I was seventeen, my friend Myles and I went to California for a surf competition. I had been competing since I was fourteen, but it was his first competition. He was so stoked because he placed eighth, which is really good for a first-timer. Anyway, to celebrate we decided to go fuck around at a beach in Laguna. It was one of the best-looking beaches I've ever surfed at." He closes his eyes as if he's picturing it in his mind. "We found a spot that looked good for diving and we took turns doing cannonballs and belly flops. Then I had the brilliant idea of jumping off backwards."

A chill sprouts across my arms as I realize where this is going.

"He got scared and I started teasing him about it. Then we started wrestling, pretending we were gonna toss each other off the cliff. Myles foot slipped. He was so startled when he began to fall backwards that he reached for my feet and hit his head on the rocky cliffside." He buries his face in his hands again, burying the shame. "It was my fault, but I panicked and called my dad before I called 9-1-1. My dad convinced me to say it was an accident."

If there is one thing that will comfort Adam right now it's for me to share my secret. It's so obvious, but I can't. I can't judge him after what I've done, but I also can't expect him not to judge me.

I put my hand under his chin and lift his face. His face is red and his eyes are brimming with unreleased tears.

"Adam, it wasn't your fault. It *was* an accident. It's not as if you pushed him off."

"That's not the point. The point is my father refused to let me tell the truth about Myles' death. And now that I'm finally getting my life back together, now that I have you, he wants to take it all away."

"You have your degree. You're young. You're smart. You're good looking. You can probably work anywhere. Why do you stay there?"

He shakes his head. "Don't you get it? The company has been in the family for more than a hundred years; started by my great-great-grandfather. Nothing is more important to my dad than the company. I can't leave. My dad has been holding what happened with Myles over my head for more than four years."

The bedroom door opens and a girl with dark-blonde hair is standing there crying with an expression of rage contorting her dainty features.

"Jamie?" Adam says as he stands from the bed.

"*You're* the reason he died?" she says, glaring at him. "I've been blaming myself for four years because I was the one who told him to enter that fucking competition and now I find out *you're* the one who pushed him off."

"I didn't push him off, Jamie. You didn't hear everything."

"I heard enough. Get the fuck out of my room!" She opens the door wide and doesn't look at me as she says,

"And take your next victim with you." Adam moves toward her and she pushes him hard in the chest. "Get out!"

Only Margaret questions why Adam and I aren't staying for the picnic, but she seems fine with Adam's explanation that he'll tell her later. The three-hour drive back to Wrightsville is filled with a silence so heavy I can barely breathe under the weight of it. I don't think anything can make this weekend worse, until I walk into my apartment and find the certified letter on the breakfast bar.

CHAPTER FOURTEEN

Relentless Demands

"THE DEPOSITS HAVE been coming for almost seventeen years, plus interest."

"How much?" I demand.

"Two hundred and seventeen thousand, two hundred twenty-nine dollars... and eight cents."

I stare at the letter on the counter sent from Northstar Bank in Raleigh notifying me of a trust account I will gain access to on my twenty-first birthday. Adam stands behind me rubbing my shoulders as I sit at the breakfast bar with my phone clutched to my ear.

After he carried the suitcase into my apartment and left me with nothing but a quick kiss on the cheek yesterday, I opened this letter and immediately called him to come back. He stayed up with me until three in the morning, though we didn't really have much to say and the curse of having a roommate-ready bedroom meant we had to sleep in separate twin beds. But right now, the sensation of his hands kneading the tension in my shoulders is enough to make me forget everything that happened at his uncle's ranch yesterday.

"My mother was not rich. This doesn't make sense. Who deposited the money into that account?"

"I can't disclose personal information about the beneficiaries, donors, or trustees over the phone. You're going to have to come in and show two forms of photo identification."

I curse myself as I think of all the times Senia begged me to renew my driver's license. "I don't have two forms of ID, unless you'll accept an expired college ID and an expired driver's license."

Henry, the bank manager, lets out an exasperated sigh. "Claire, only because I knew your mother and how much she loved you will I allow this. Come in on your birthday with both your expired IDs and another person with two valid forms of ID and I'll give you what you need."

I hang up the phone feeling lost. I grew up in a tiny rundown trailer on a lot surrounded by acres of forest. Our nearest neighbor must have been at least a quarter mile away because it felt like it took a million years to get there on foot every time we visited "Grandma" Patty. Nothing about the way we lived gave me any indication that my mother had money, but what Henry just said to me didn't imply that she did. He said the deposits had been coming in for almost seventeen years. My mother has been dead for more than thirteen years. Someone else was making those deposits.

Once I tell Adam the stipulations, he quickly offers to go with me to Raleigh for my birthday. "That's perfect because the birthday present I want to give you is in Raleigh."

I don't bother asking what he's getting me because I know he'll only refuse to tell me, but I'm more than a little apprehensive about turning twenty-one now.

I twist around on the barstool so I'm facing him and I can see the insecurity in his eyes—the look that's been there since we left his uncle's house yesterday. He's wondering if I'm judging him because of what happened to his friend Myles four years ago.

"I'm sorry about what happened to your friend. And I'm sorry you've had to live with that for four years. But most of all, I'm sorry that I can't share my secret with you the way you've shared yours with me." He shakes his head and opens his mouth to say something, but I press a shaky finger to his lips. "But I want you to know that I do love you. And it scares the hell out of me to feel this way about someone I've known all of three weeks."

He grabs my hand and moves my finger away from his lips. "It doesn't have to make sense; it only has to make you happy. Are you happy?"

I grab the front of his T-shirt and pull him closer so my knees are hugging his hips. "I'm happier than a pig in mud."

He smiles as he grabs the sides of my waist. "You've been spending too much time with Cora?"

I gaze into his eyes willing him to hear my thoughts. He stares back at me, a bit confused at first by my intense gaze, but then he sees it. He crushes his lips against mine and opens his mouth slowly. The pressure and heat of his lips sends a wave of chills coursing through me and I wrap my arms and legs around him, pulling him closer.

His hands slide under my shirt to undo my bra as he kisses my neck. As soon as the snap breaks loose, I peel off my shirt and bra and toss them onto the carpet. I lean my back against the cool tile of the breakfast bar and he takes my nipple into his mouth as he rolls my other nipple between his fingertips. I tighten my legs around his waist as the moisture builds between my thighs. He slides his hands under my butt and lifts me off the barstool. I kiss him greedily as he carries me to the bedroom.

He sits me down on the edge of the bed and stands so he can peel his shirt off as I undo the button and zipper on his cargo shorts. His erection is a massive bulge under his boxer briefs. I want to unwrap it, but I'm a bit frightened by the size of that bulge. He must see the apprehension in my face because he chooses to leave his briefs on for the time being as he kneels before me.

"Stand up," he demands.

He slowly removes my shorts and panties as he plants a soft kiss on each of my hips. He presses his lips to my stomach just underneath my belly button and my nipples instantly stiffen. Taking my hand in his, he lays a soft kiss on my knuckles as he looks up at me.

"Sit down," he murmurs, and I quickly obey. As soon as I'm seated on the edge of the bed, he spreads my legs and kisses the inside of my knee. "I love you, Claire. I want to make you happier than you've ever been."

He lays a trail of kisses over the inside of both my thighs before he rests my legs on top of his shoulders and goes straight for my aching clit.

"Oh, Adam," I moan.

He kisses and licks me slowly, taking his time, savoring every inch of me as I arch my back. He thrusts two fingers inside me and massages me to the same rhythm of his tongue. My arms begin to weaken from leaning back on my hands. I lower myself down to my elbows as his tongue swirls around my clit and my hips buck against his fingers.

"I'm gonna come," I whimper. "Don't stop."

The orgasm rolls through me like the sizzle of a fuse being lit followed by an intense explosion of pleasure. He grips my thighs tightly, not pulling his mouth away until my body stops convulsing. He lets my legs slide off his shoulders as his chest glides over me. He kisses me hard and I can taste the coffee we drank this morning and myself. His tongue thrusts in and out of my mouth and I grab his perfect ass to pull him down on top of me.

"Please," I whisper into his mouth as I reach down and slide my hand inside his briefs.

"Oh, fuck," he whispers as I get a firm grip on the base of his cock and slide my hand down to feel the length of it.

I pull my hand out and scoot up the bed to sit on my knees as I point at the pillow. "Lay down."

He smiles as he slides his briefs off and I finally glimpse his full erection as he lies before me, his body glistening with sweat. My heart thumps against my chest as I realize I haven't done this in so long and I've only done it with Chris. I don't even know if I'm any good at it, but I know I want to do it. That has to count for something.

I slide his legs apart and position myself cross-legged between his legs as if I'm about to meditate. I wrap my fingers around the head then slide my hand down to stretch the skin taut. God, it looks perfect. I lean over and lick around the ridge, tasting his slight saltiness. He groans and I lick my lips before I wrap them around the head. I swirl my tongue over the tip before I take him further into my mouth. I close my eyes and hum softly as he hits the back of my throat.

He sucks in a sharp breath through his teeth as his fingers slide over my head and grip a handful of hair. "Oh, baby."

I slide him out slowly and kiss the tip before I take him into my mouth again and bob my head; slowly at first then I pick up speed. I use my other hand to massage his pulsating sac. He's panting and moaning and I'm drunk on the power of having this effect on him. I don't want to stop, but I soon feel his sac contracting in my hand. His hips thrust gently, his fingers tugging my hair, as he lets go in my mouth.

He's softening as I slide him out and swipe my thumb across the corner of my mouth. My body is shaking with adrenaline as he sits up and takes my face in his hands. He kisses me hungrily as I climb onto his lap. He pulls his head back and rests his forehead against mine, his chest heaving as he lets out a low chuckle.

"You are so sexy. How did I get so lucky?"

"You stalked the crap out of me."

He laughs as he reaches over the side of the bed and picks his shorts up off the floor. He digs through his pocket and pulls out his wallet. I look on impatiently as he tosses the condom wrapper and the wallet onto the floor and slides the condom on.

He slides his finger into my folds and massages my clit as he kisses my neck. "You drive me so fuckin' crazy," he breathes into my ear as he takes my earlobe between his teeth and a shock of pleasure pulsates between my legs. "Come for me, baby."

I grind my hips as he caresses me, arching my back and

he takes my nipple into his mouth, sucking and tugging at the sensitive flesh. I lose myself again and the cry that's been building in my throat releases as I collapse in his arms. He flips me gently onto my back and positions himself between my legs. He sinks down onto his elbows so our noses are touching then slowly guides himself into me, not giving me any time to recover. I gasp and he stops.

"Are you okay?"

"Yes, yes, yes. Don't stop."

It's painful, but definitely worth it as he slides farther into me until he hits my core. I let out an involuntary whimper and he swallows it as he kisses me tenderly, dipping in and out of me. His chest rubs against mine, sending sparks through my sensitive nipples, and I moan into his mouth. He pierces me steadily as he gently stretches me.

"I love you so much," he murmurs as he looks into my eyes.

"I love you, too." I hold his gaze and rock my hips in rhythm with his thrusts.

He kisses me again, hungrier this time as I rake my nails softly over his back. His arms begin to shake as he reaches climax. He lingers inside me as he kisses me, drawing out the moment. Finally, he pulls away and plants a kiss on my lips and another on my nose before he rolls off me.

I stare at the ceiling in a daze. I did it. And it was

amazing. This must mean I'm over him. I don't even want to think his name. I don't want to think about what I did to him. I turn my head and Adam looks exhausted, but he's still smiling and beckoning me to curl up next to him.

This is me turning the page on another chapter.

CHAPTER FIFTEEN

Relentless Secrets

TWO WEEKS TICK by like seconds on a clock, and before we know it it's the Thursday night before my birthday. Adam and I have spent the past twelve days checking in on Cora; taking group surf lessons with other beginners on Shell Island; and carefully avoiding the subject of why I dropped out of school and what those house plans on his drafting table are for. We've exchanged house keys, but we still haven't exchanged secrets. It should serve as some sort of warning that there are still some things we haven't shared with each other, but I try not to let it bother me and I assume he's doing the same.

Adam sits on his sofa and I sit next to him with my handful of Red Vines. "Jamie called me last night to apologize for kicking us out of her room. It only took her, what, two weeks?"

"Did you guys talk about it?" I ask as I take a bite of my licorice and hand him one.

He waves away the candy. "Yeah. It was nice. We used to have long talks all the time when her and Myles were together. Nothing was the same after he died."

I lay my cheek against his soft T-shirt and inhale the fresh laundry fragrance combined with his warm man scent.

"Are you sniffing me again?"

"I can't help it. You smell so delicious."

He points the remote at the TV and the channel changes multiple times until he settles on MTV.

"I can guarantee you I taste better than I smell," he says and I smack his chest. "Just making it known in case you get any ideas."

I lean my head back and he looks down at me with that hungry look I've come to know so well. The look that can make me do things I would never do.

I clasp my hands around the back of his neck and pull his face toward me. As our lips touch, the host on MTV announces, "And now, the highly anticipated world premiere video from Chris Knight's debut album *Relentless*. Here is "SLEEPYHEAD"!"

"Come here," he growls as his hands slide over my ass and he pulls me up so I'm straddling him.

I press my hands against his chest and push off. I can feel him underneath me, but I can't see him and I realize it's because my eyes are closed as the memory slams into me.

Chris's lips smell and taste like the berry Capri-Sun he was just sipping and I can't shake the feeling that we're too young to be alone in my room. But it feels so right as his fingers lightly graze my ribs sending chills through every part of my body. I'm eighteen today. Eighteen is a perfectly fine age to lose your virginity; especially if it's with the boyfriend you've been with for more than two years, who also happens to be the most amazing, patient boyfriend a girl could ask for.

His hand slides farther up and I flinch when his fingers hit the wire of my bra. "I love you," he whispers, and somehow this has the opposite effect.

I push him off and he sighs as he lies back. "I'm sorry," I mutter. "I'm just scared that it's going to hurt and then I'll feel different about you. I don't want to feel like you've hurt me."

He turns onto his side and kisses my cheek. He slips his hand under my T-shirt and traces circles around my belly button as he says, "I could never hurt you. You're my Claire-bear. But I can't fucking lie. I want to be inside you so bad... I want to make you feel as good as you make me feel." He plants a soft kiss on my belly and I shiver. "But I'll wait as long as it takes."

I stroke his hair out of his face and whisper, "I love you."

He kisses my temple before he springs up off the bed, leaving me feeling a little used up. "I'll be right back, babe."

He comes back a minute later with his acoustic guitar and closes the bedroom door. No one else is home. Jackie and her new boyfriend Tim are running errands before we meet them tonight for a birthday dinner. If Jackie knew what Chris and I are doing right now she'd kill both of us. Somehow, we've managed to keep our relationship a secret from her. This makes it seem as if Chris and I are doing something wrong, though we're not.

The simple gesture of Chris closing the bedroom door makes me feel safe, like he knows exactly what I need. He always has.

I scoot back so he can sit on the edge of the bed next to me. He settles down with his guitar in his lap and strums a haphazard melody as he tunes the guitar by ear.

"I wrote this for you. It's about the day we met. It's called 'Sleepyhead'."

I smile as I remember how tired I was the day we met from not having slept the night before, but somehow he still convinced me to go downstairs and listen to him play.

His lips start toying with the ball piercing in his tongue, the way they always do when he's working up the nerve to perform for me. He claims it's unintentional, but it's extremely hot. He starts plucking the strings and the melody that flows out is both haunting and sweet. I'm already on the verge of tears when he begins to sing.

"Feels so wrong to want this. You look so broken there. A flicker in the mist, as tired as the air." He looks up at me and my breath hitches. He holds my gaze the entire time he's singing, except when he closes his eyes as he belts out the chorus. "So frightened of the dark. You're my sleepyhead. Hiding with the stars. Put your dreams to bed, my sleepyhead."

A tear rolls down my cheek and falls on his guitar as I grab his face and kiss him.

I open my eyes and Adam's face is blurry through the tears.

"Claire, why are you crying?" Adam asks as he takes the Red Vines from my hand and lays them on the coffee table.

"I'm sorry," I whisper, wiping my cheeks as the song continues to play in the background. I scoot over to the other end of the sofa and hug my knees tightly. "I'm a horrible, horrible person."

"Don't say that."

"It's true."

I can feel him staring at me, but I keep my gaze focused on the ropes of red licorice on the table. They remind me of blood vessels and I think of how my mother abused her veins. I think of how I nearly took a razor to my veins six months ago. I think of all the secrets pumping through my veins, poisoning me, ruining me.

"There are some things that, no matter how hard you try to convince yourself they're for the best, always seem to cut a chunk out of your heart. And you know that no matter how many wonderful people and beautiful adventures you welcome into your life, you'll never be whole again. You'll never be you again." My throat aches as I speak, but I keep going. "I don't even know who I was before I dropped out. I feel like that person wasn't me. Or maybe who I am now isn't the real me. All I know is that I became the kind of person I always swore I would never be, and from here on out that will never change because no amount of apologizing can undo what I did."

He scoots toward me and I ball myself up tighter. "Claire." Just the way he says my name makes me bristle. I know he's going to tell me something I don't want to hear. I close my eyes as he says, "I know what it's like to feel like the guilt will destroy you. Those plans you found the other day, the day we left to go to my uncle's house, those plans are a manifestation of my guilt."

I open my eyes and he's staring at the drafting table in the corner of the room with a distant look in his eyes. He rises from the sofa and wanders toward the corner where he lifts a few sets of plans off the top of the stack and slides the house plans out from the bottom. He comes back to the sofa and lays the plans on the coffee table in front of us.

"Myles' family never had a lot of money. His dad was always too busy getting on with his new family; he never really supported Myles or his mom and two sisters." He flips the top sheet and a floor plan of the house is laid out before us. "I've been designing this house for the past three years with the idea that one day I'll be able to build it for them. Maybe then I won't feel like I took away the one shot they had at a decent future." He lets out a low laugh as he shakes his head. "My dad found these plans and now he's holding my trust fund until I turn thirty so I can't build it. He thinks it would be like admitting my guilt. He doesn't understand that that's exactly what this house is. It's an apology and an admission. I can't live with this anymore."

He finally turns to me and I can see the agony he's carrying. I draw in a shaky breath as he looks me in the eye, his eyes searching for a sliver of understanding. I want to tell him everything. He's shared so much of himself with me. He needs to know the kind of person I am. He deserves to know the kind of person he fell in love with.

But I can't.

I cover my face with my hands; afraid he'll see the razors of shame shredding my insides. These jagged lies I've told myself for the past year have rested comfortably beneath the delicate skin of truth. I can't allow them to pierce through to the surface. I can't allow myself to become a bloody mess again.

I need to meditate.

I stand quickly from the sofa and his eyes follow me as I walk toward the door.

"Where are you going?"

"I have to go."

He darts toward the front door and blocks it off as I reach for the doorknob. "You can't keep pushing this down or it's going to burn you from the inside out. Forget the fucking bet. I don't care about that. Just please talk to me."

I stare at the buttons on his shirt. I rarely see him wearing his work clothes in his apartment. He usually changes before I make it upstairs. He actually wrangled Linda into giving me today, tomorrow, and Saturday off for my birthday. I've never had three days off from the café. Adam can convince just about anyone to do just about anything, but he can't convince himself that he's not to blame for Myles' death and he can't convince me to spill my guts to him.

"Fucking shit, Claire!" he groans as I remain silent. "You're self-medicating with that meditation shit. You might as well be shooting heroin in your veins. You're numb and you can't even see it."

"I can't believe you would even say that."

"Yes, your mother died of a drug overdose and it's tragic and I wish I could take your pain and make it my own, but I can't. And you have to understand that your mother loved you. She wouldn't have been so careful about keeping you safe if she didn't love you. She made a mistake, but that's because she was sick. You're not sick, Claire. You're just heartbroken."

I reach for the door and he pushes my hand away. "Please get out of my way."

My whole body is trembling with all the horrible things I want to shout at him, but I can't let myself lose control. His face is twisted with pity, but he doesn't move.

"I'm not moving until you talk to me."

"I don't want to talk. Please get out of my way."

"No."

I push him hard in the chest and he grabs my wrist. "Get out of my fucking way!" I try to wrench my arms free, but he pulls me against him so I can't get any leverage. "Let go."

"Is that what you want? You want me to let this go? You want me to watch you suffer like this? Because I can't do it anymore."

He lets go of my wrists and I'm stunned into silence. The one thing he wants is the one thing I can't give.

"You think I can't see it? You think I can't see that I'm sinking like a stone and no one, not even you, can rescue me?" I whisper as I clutch my fists to my chest. "This was inevitable. You don't want to know what I did. Trust me when I say that. If I tell you what I did you will never trust me again... and I don't think I could handle that. So I guess it's best if we just stop before we're in too deep."

"It's too late for that," he says, his voice sounding too thick. "I can't believe you're willing to throw this all away because you think I'm going to judge you or stop trusting you—especially after everything you've learned about me." He reaches for my face and I swallow hard as I try to hold back my tears. "Look at this face." He strokes my cheekbones with his thumbs. "How could I ever not trust this face? Or these eyes?" He kisses both my eyelids, and my throat aches with all the words I wish I could say. "And these lips... How could I ever curse a single word that comes out of these lips?"

He kisses me so tenderly I sob softly into his mouth. He pulls away and I know I probably look like a mess.

"I just need to be alone for a little while," I say in a strangled whisper.

He nods and kisses my forehead. "I'll come by later to check on you."

I nod as I reach for the doorknob again and he places his hand over mine. "Maybe you'll get some answers when we go to Raleigh tomorrow. Maybe your heart will be a little less broken once we leave there."

I don't have it in me to tell him that this trust account has nothing to do with my broken heart so I just nod. He kisses my temple once more before I leave. As I descend the steps to my apartment, only one thought occupies my troubled mind: It's time to call Jackie Knight.

CHAPTER SIXTEEN

Relentless Signs

I WAKE UP to total darkness with my leg curled around Adam's leg and my cheek plastered to his stomach. This humidity is becoming too much. The impending tropical storm set to hit the Carolinas tonight is not helping any. I peel my face off his belly and he reaches down to take my face in his hands. He pulls my lips to his and sucks gently on my bottom lip.

"Mmm…" He moans as I lay on top of him. "Happy birthday, babydoll."

He kisses me hard and I feel him growing beneath me. He flips me onto my back and I come down so hard on the mattress that the two twin beds we pushed together in my bedroom nearly split apart underneath me. We both laugh as we scoot over so we're not on the crack. He leans in to kiss my neck and I skim my fingers down his washboard abs and grab his hard length.

He moves my hand away as he slithers down and takes my nipple into his mouth, teasing my nipple with his tongue and giving it a soft tug. He moves to my other breast and I grab a fistful of his hair to pull him up. I kiss him hungrily as I wrap my legs around his waist.

"It's your birthday," he says between kisses. "I'll do whatever you want." His tongue slides into my mouth and I suck on it for a bit before he pulls back. "Let me eat you up. You'll be my slice of birthday cake."

"We don't have much time. We have to go to the bank. Let's multitask and do it in the shower."

He grins at me as he kisses the tip of my nose. "So efficient. But we have plenty of time. The sun hasn't even come up yet."

I turn toward the window then back to him. "Why are we up so early?"

"I wanted to wake you up in time for your favorite time of day."

He slides down my body and lays a soft kiss between my legs before he rises from the bed. A shiver travels over my thighs and I press my legs together to stop myself from pulling him back on top of me this instant.

We go outside and sit on the bottom of the steps that lead to his apartment as we wait for that golden moment just before the sun comes up.

That's when he turns to me and whispers in my ear, "I

promise today will be the best birthday you've ever had."

WHEN THE WATER in the shower begins to run cold, we drag ourselves out of the shower and take our time drying each other off.

"Wear some comfortable shoes today. No heels." He gently tugs the brush through my hair as we stand in front of the bathroom mirror. He always wants to brush my hair now that he knows it sends chills through my entire body. "I have a birthday surprise for you and I want you to be comfortable."

"A surprise for me in Raleigh? You're not taking me dancing or to a club, are you? I hate clubs."

The brush catches on a knot in my hair and I yelp. "Sorry! No, it's not a club." He kisses the top of my head and hands me the brush. "You finish making yourself pretty and I'll finish making you breakfast."

Adam considers himself a gourmet chef now that I've taught him how to make my favorite fruit and yogurt parfait for breakfast. He keeps both of our refrigerators stocked with yogurt and fruit and makes it for me, along with my favorite kind of coffee, every time we spend the night together. I don't have the heart to tell him I'm getting sick of it.

An hour later, I emerge from the bathroom fully primped and dressed in a thin, butter-yellow, off-the-shoulder shirt over a camisole and some white jean shorts. And, as Adam requested, I'm wearing some gladiator sandals with no heels. He looks me up and down as I step out of the bedroom while pulling on a silver bangle bracelet Senia gave me for President's Day. She insists all holidays are an excuse to give gifts.

I pull my phone out of my back pocket to text her as Adam pushes a bowl of fruit and yogurt across the breakfast bar toward me. I smile at him as I punch in a message asking if she's still meeting Adam and me for an early dinner at Bida Manda. I place my phone next to my bowl of yogurt and take the first bite of yogurt with a chunk of pineapple.

"Mmm…"

Adam smiles then plants a firm kiss on my temple before he heads for the door. "I'm going upstairs to get dressed. I'll be back faster than you can say Bida Manda."

"You read my text!" I shriek, and he cackles as he dashes out the front door.

As soon as the door closes, I pick up my phone and scroll through my contacts for Jackie Knight. I don't hesitate and within two rings she answers.

"Hello?"

She sounds exactly the same as she did a year ago when I told her I was moving out of the dorm, promising to give her my new phone number once I was settled. Her voice still had that faint Southern accent she had tried to snuff out during her college years in Arizona.

"Jackie?" My voice is shaky and a bit thick with phlegm from the yogurt. I clear my throat and I hear a sharp intake of breath on the other end of the line. "Jackie, it's Claire."

"I know," she whispers, and now it's obvious she's crying and it instantly makes me want to cry.

"Jackie, I'm so sorry I haven't called."

"Are you okay? Please tell me you're okay."

"I'm fine. I promise. I'm okay."

"Oh, thank God." She whispers this a few more times and my chest aches with the thought of what I've put her through.

She *doesn't* hate me.

"Claire, honey, please tell me you're coming home for your birthday."

"Not tonight. I have plans. But I'm staying the night in Raleigh and I want to come see you in the morning. Is that okay?"

"Is that *okay*? Honey, you don't have to ask if you can come here. This is your home. You are always welcome here."

For a moment, I can't breathe. I'm reminded of how much I loved living with Chris and Jackie. Even the boyfriends Jackie dated were always sweet and respectful. She never settled down after divorcing Chris's father when he was six. She always insisted she was too picky, but the truth is she's too strong-minded and independent. She won't take shit from anybody, which is why I fully expected her to be pissed at me. This tearful acceptance is possibly worse.

"I'll be there in the morning," I say as the front door opens and Adam walks in wearing jeans and a black Rip Curl T-shirt that hugs his ripped chest.

"Claire?"

"Yeah?"

"I can't wait to see you."

"Me, too," I whisper before I hang up.

Adam waits for me by the door wearing a crooked smile that melts my heart. I tuck my phone into my back pocket and stuff my two expired IDs into my other back pocket. I go to him and wrap my arms around his waist as I rest my cheek against his chest.

"Thank you for taking me today."

"I haven't even taken you yet. How do you know this isn't an elaborate ruse to get my hands on your trust fund?"

I lean my head back and look into his eyes, ready to butter him up. "You have the most gorgeous light-green eyes I have ever seen on a human being."

"That's because they're full of dollar signs."

"If I give you all my money, can you take me to see my foster mother tomorrow morning?"

"Tell you what, I'll let you keep the money if you let me have an extra slice of birthday cake tonight."

"Deal."

"And you know what I mean when I say birthday cake."

"Of course I do. That stuff with the frosting."

He leans down to kiss me, stopping right before our lips touch. "The frosting's the best part."

AFTER CHECKING IN on Cora, we hop into the truck with no suitcase this time. Adam insists we can sleep naked in the hotel room and I really have no problem with this suggestion.

All the local radio stations seem to be obsessed with playing Chris Knight songs this morning so I'm extremely grateful when Adam lets me put my music on again. I need to listen to something that will calm my nerves. I find an old classical music playlist I made for meditating and hit play.

"Really?" he asks, cocking an eyebrow as he casts me a sideways glance.

"I haven't meditated today. I need something to help me relax."

"Only because it's your birthday." We sit in silence for a few minutes before he sighs. "Claire, I need to ask you something."

"Sounds serious."

"This foster mother we're going to see tomorrow…

does she know why you dropped out of UNC?"

"She doesn't even know I dropped out."

"Oh."

He's silent for a moment and I take the opportunity to gaze at all the highway signage displaying all the names of streets I haven't seen since before Senia moved in. It's been more than three months since I've been to Raleigh. Every mile we drive brings me closer to knowing the truth about the trust fund my mother left me, and closer to the lies I've been running from for the past year.

"Can I ask you something else?" he says, and something about the way his voice goes a little too high on the last word makes me think he's nervous about this question.

"Go ahead."

"This guy that you were with before me, what was his name again?"

"I never told you his name."

"Right. Well, does he live in Raleigh?"

I pause as I try to figure out where this is going. Does he want to know if there's a chance we may run into Chris or does he want to track him down and try to find out my secret from him? Or, maybe, he thinks Chris is the one who broke my heart and he wants to beat the shit out of him. I'm going to assume it's the first one. That's the safest conclusion to jump to.

"We're not going to run into him. He left Raleigh right

after we broke up last year."

"Did you break up with him?"

He's fishing. He's asked similar, but more vague, questions over the past few weeks, but they've been ambiguous enough for me to dodge them or answer them without giving too much away. For instance, last week he asked if I had ever been cheated on. A few days before that he asked how many guys I've had sex with. When I told him I've only had sex with one other guy, he got a glimmer of hope in his eye. He seemed to be pleased to know that I'm practically virginal and to have me just a little more figured out.

"Yes, I broke up with him."

"This is the same guy who was your first?"

"Why are you asking these questions all of a sudden?"

"I just feel like I should know these things before we get to your 'hood. I'm not a Raleigh guy. I grew up in and around Carolina Beach before my parents moved to Wilmington five years ago when I went to Duke. I don't have a lot of friends in Raleigh. I just want to make sure I'm not caught by surprise."

He thinks we're going to run into someone, not just Chris, who may give him a hard time about being with me. Maybe he even thinks Jackie's going to give him a hard time. He may be right about that. When Chris and I broke the news about our relationship to Jackie shortly after my eighteenth birthday, she wasn't surprised—she was ecstatic.

Something tells me she won't be so ecstatic to see me with Adam.

"Look. When we go to my foster mother's house tomorrow, you're going to have to stay in the truck. I really wish I could introduce you to her, but I just don't think it's the right time."

"Really?"

"Really. She doesn't know I dropped out. She doesn't know what happened after I dropped out. And she doesn't know about you. She's very protective and opinionated. I have a lot to talk about with her tomorrow. I want to ease her into everything that's happened. I don't want her to dislike you just because she's pissed at me."

He raises his eyebrows as he keeps his eyes on the road stretched out before us like a silver sword delivering us into the belly of the beast. He's not pleased with my explanation of why he can't meet Jackie. But this is only because he doesn't understand that I'm saving him the grief of too much information. The less he knows about who Jackie is, the less he knows about who Chris is. The less Adam knows about Chris, the less chance he'll have of being intimidated by the fact that not only is Chris Knight my ex, but I'm the inspiration for so many of the Chris Knight songs he loves.

I take a deep breath and prepare myself to make the biggest mistake I've made in a very long time. "Okay. How about this? When we get home tomorrow I'll tell you everything—but not until then. I just want to enjoy my birthday."

"You don't have to do that."

"I know I don't. I want to." Just speaking these words aloud dials up the anxiety inside me and I draw in another deep breath. "I need to."

He reaches across the console and grabs my hand. "I'm ready when you are."

CHAPTER SEVENTEEN

Relentless Revelations

WE WALK INTO Northstar Bank and I instantly remember it. I remember the lobby with the speckled brown tiles, the high ceiling, and the enormous wood and glass chandelier. I remember the offices to my left where my mom brought me once when I was six or seven. Did she bring me with her when she set up the trust account?

I walk through the doorway on my left into another small reception area and the receptionist looks up from her computer screen with her eyebrows raised and lips pursed as if my mere presence annoys her.

"Can I help you?" she finally says.

I try not to roll my eyes as I say, "I'm here to see Henry Owens."

"Is he expecting you?"

"I'm pretty sure he's been expecting me for thirteen

years."

She picks up her phone and dials an extension. "Henry, you have…"

"Claire Nixon," I say as she looks up at me questioningly.

"…Claire Nixon here to see you." She glances at my shorts quickly as she listens to Henry speak. "Got it." She hangs up and the smug look on her face makes me dread what she's about to say. "He's in the middle of something. He said you'll have to wait a while since you don't have an *appointment*."

This time I can't stop myself from rolling my eyes as I turn around and take a seat next to Adam on the tweed armchairs that look like they've been here since the eighties.

Adam grabs my hand and gives it a squeeze. "You've waited thirteen years. You can wait a few more minutes."

"Take your wisdom and get outta here."

He smiles and kisses my cheek. "Want to hear a joke while you wait?"

Honestly, I'm already nervous as hell. I don't think a corny joke is going to calm my nerves, but I can't resist the urge to hear him bomb. I look at him for a moment before I answer because I can't believe how lucky I am. Some moments are made for showing us who our true friends are, and in this moment I realize Adam is my friend. My true friend. He drove 135 miles to prove that to me today. I don't feel like I deserve him, but I'll do my best to keep him. And someday I'll find a way to repay him.

"Go for it," I say.

He squints at me because he knows my mind is elsewhere. "Okay. Dirty or corny?"

I glance at the receptionist who appears to be enthralled in whatever she's looking at on her computer screen, but she's only eight feet away.

"Better go for corny this time," I mutter.

"Okay. Knock, knock."

"Who's there?"

"Olive."

"Olive who?"

"Olive You."

"I think I just threw up some fruit and yogurt in my mouth." His eyes widen as he pretends to be offended and I smile. "Where are my manners? Come on in. I've been waiting for you all my life, Olive You."

"You're not just saying that 'cause I said it, are you?"

"Nope. I mean it. Honestly and truly. Olive You with all my mushy red pimiento heart."

"Now *I* just threw up in my mouth." He grins as he leans in to kiss me then I hear someone call my name. I turn and find a thin gentleman, maybe late-forties, with graying brown hair, a gray suit, and a kind face.

"Are you ready, Claire?" he asks, and I nod as I rise from the chair.

Adam stays close behind as I follow Henry down a

corridor of cubicles. He turns right at the end of the corridor and heads for an open office door. We enter the office and he waves at a couple of chairs identical to the ones in the lobby. He takes a seat in his leather desk chair and rests his elbows on top of a manila folder in the center of his desk.

"First of all, Claire, I just want to say that I'm very sorry about your mother. She was a friend of mine in high school and I was devastated to hear about her death and even more saddened to know the circumstances."

He's probably referring to the fact that I was locked in that trailer with my dead mother for nearly two days. I should be angry that he's brought this image into my mind, but he does look genuinely saddened.

"Thank you," I say. "But I'm not here to talk about my mother's death. I'm here to talk about this trust account. I want to know where the money came from."

"Of course. Do you mind closing the door?" he asks Adam, who's closest to the office door.

Adam doesn't even have to stand from his chair in this tiny office to push the door softly closed.

Henry opens the manila folder and his eyes scan the contents as he flips through the pages. "I have hundreds of deposits here. They're all electronic funds transfers from a single donor."

"Not my mother?"

He shakes his head solemnly and I almost want to

reach across the desk and strangle him to spit it out.

"Who?" I ask as I lean forward in my chair.

"I'll need to see some identification first, as we discussed."

I look over my shoulder at Adam and he pulls out his wallet as I slide my two expired IDs out of my back pocket. I lay them flat on the desk and Adam lays his driver's license and a credit card next to mine. Henry examines all four IDs for a moment before he slides them back across the desk.

"Well, as I'm sure you've guessed, your mother is the grantor for the trust and she requested that you not be granted access until your twenty-first birthday." He heaves a sigh as he gazes at the folder in front of him. "She wanted you to be provided for."

The way he says this makes me think my mother knew she wasn't going to live very long. I'm sure most drug addicts feel this way at some point, but something feels off about this whole situation.

"Are you saying my mom killed herself?"

Henry looks up from the folder looking confused. He thought I already knew this.

"Oh, God," I whisper as I bury my face in my hands. "I can't believe this."

"Your mother loved you, Claire," Henry insists.

Adam rubs my back as I press the heels of my hands against my eyelids; trying to push back the memory of the hours I spent hiding from my mother's dead body. I think of how my legs ached as I stood in the crack between the refrigerator and the wall. How I convinced myself more than once that if I came out of my hiding place, this time she would be alive. How I pissed myself because I was too afraid to walk through the living room to go to the restroom. How the policeman who found me cried as he carried me out of the trailer. All this time I thought it was an accident. I thought my mother made a mistake, a miscalculation. Even after everything I went through before that policeman found me and in all the foster homes after that, I never hated my mother. Until now.

I sit up and wipe the tears away from my face. "Who's the donor?"

The lines at the corners of his eyes deepen as he contemplates the answer to this question. He glances at Adam then back at me. "I think you might want to be alone when you hear this."

Adam begins to stand and I put my hand on his knee to stop him. "Henry, you just told me my mother committed suicide," I say incredulously. "Do you really think anything you tell me now is going to be more devastating than that? Who's the fucking donor?"

Henry looks back and forth nervously between Adam and me as if we've just pointed guns at his head and asked him to open the bank vault. "Yes, I do think this news will be quite devastating, but I'll respect your wishes if you want your friend here with you." My leg starts bouncing uncontrollably as I wait for Henry's next words. "Your father is the donor, but—" He puts a hand up to stop me from speaking when I open my mouth. "—before you accuse your mother of keeping you from your father while taking his money, there's something you need to know."

The few bites of yogurt I ate three hours ago are swirling in my belly as my stomach twists in knots from the anticipation.

"Claire, your mother was raped when she was seventeen by one of her cousins."

I knew her uncle repeatedly raped her from age nine to fourteen, but she never told me anything about her cousin.

"Are you sure you don't mean she was raped by her uncle? Because she told me about that."

Henry shakes his head. "It was the son of the same uncle. Claire, your mother was a good person. She trusted too many people too much."

"Until she didn't trust anybody at all," I say, beginning to understand why my mother kept me locked away in that trailer and why she was so adamant about teaching me how to stay safe.

Then another realization hits me. We were talking about the donor on the trust account before Henry told me my mother was raped by her cousin.

"Oh, God," I whisper, and I double over in my chair, suddenly feeling as if a ten-ton slab of concrete is crushing my chest. "He's my father."

Adam slides off the chair and kneels in front of me. "I think we should leave." He lifts my chin and takes my face in his hands. "You don't need to hear any more of this shit."

"My mother never told me any of this," I whisper as he swipes his thumb across my face to brush away the tears. "He raped her and she still took his money."

I grab Adam's hands and pull them away from my face, but I hold tight to them as they rest in my lap.

"She did it because she wanted you to be taken care of," Henry insists.

"Two hundred and seventeen thousand dollars." Just saying the words aloud makes me feel filthy. "Why would he give her so much money?"

Almost as soon as I speak the words I know the answer. It was hush money to keep her from turning him in. It had to be. She used her pain to extort money from him. She gave up the chance for justice so that I would have a chance at a better life.

"I don't want that money."

Adam stares fiercely into my eyes. "You don't have to take a single penny of it. Let's get out of here. You don't need this shit, especially not on your birthday."

"You know we can't legally keep this money. The money will just sit here collecting interest," Henry informs me, as if I care. "She *wanted* you to have the money."

Adam stands up and scoots aside so I can stand. Henry looks up at me from his desk with a sad look in his eyes. He's disappointed that I can't take the money my mother intended for me. I wonder silently if he ever had a relationship with my mother. How could someone so kind and straight-laced as Henry be so fiercely protective of a heroin addict who committed suicide and extorted money from her rapist?

I know my mother had a hard life. I didn't know anyone who'd had a more difficult life than her. But that was no excuse for what she did. She left me homeless, drifting from one family to the next, never staying anywhere long enough to form any true friendships. Maybe she thought she was doing me a favor by tearing herself out of my life. Maybe she thought I would end up with a good family right away. She didn't know it would take eight years for me to arrive on the Knights' doorstep.

"I just have one more question," I say as Adam and I reach the office door. "If my mom knew she was going to kill herself, why didn't she call the police before she did it? Why didn't she send me to Patty's house or something? Why did she make me stay there with her?"

Henry heaves a deep sigh. "I don't know."

"ARE YOU SURE you still want to go to dinner? We can stay

at the hotel room and talk. Or we can go home. It's up to you."

I shake my head and close my eyes as I lean back against the headrest in the truck. "I don't want to make any more decisions today. You decide."

"Okay, we're going home."

"No! I want to see Senia tonight. Just go to the hotel and we can hang out there until dinner."

"Anything you want."

After we check in at the hotel, we go up to our room and curl up on the bed.

"I want to know what it's like to not feel lost," I say as I rest my head on Adam's shoulder and he strokes my hair.

"I don't know if anybody ever gets there, but we can try."

"My mom and I used to play this game whenever someone knocked on our front door. She would face the door while I chose one of three hiding places: under the bed, in the closet, or in the nook between the fridge and the wall. As soon as she got rid of whoever was at the door, she'd come looking for me. If I was hiding in the first place she looked, she got to tickle me. I think of stuff like that then I think of the things Henry just told me and I don't think I ever knew my mother."

"None of this has to make any sense to you right now."

"The thing is, it *does* make sense. She didn't want to

live. I almost don't blame her for ending her life after everything she went through." I curl my fingers around a piece of his shirt and squeeze tightly. "The worst part is that I still want her here. Even after everything I've learned today. And part of me knows that if I had been braver, if I had called 9-1-1 right away, she might still be here."

"You don't know that. You said it yourself; you don't blame her after everything she went through. If you had saved her that day, she probably would have found another way to do it."

I don't say anything because he's right. My mother didn't want to live, not even for me.

"I'm just so angry with her."

"One thing they taught us in anger management—"

"Oh, no," I mutter.

He pokes my side and continues his pep talk over my laughter. "Go ahead laugh, but I'm serious. I know you like to meditate, but they taught us in anger management class to let go of the anger by imagining what you would say to the person you're angry with if you forgave them. What would you say to your mom to let her know you've forgiven her?"

I pause for a moment to think about this. There are so many things I'd say to her. I've spent countless nights lying in bed unable to sleep as I imagine the conversations we'd have if she were still alive.

I sit up on the bed and cross my legs as if I'm going to

meditate. "I would tell her that I love her and that I know she did what she thought she needed to do to make the aching go away. I would tell her that I'm sorry about what happened to her and how I wish I was the one who could have healed her."

Adam sits up and grabs my hands. "What else?"

"I'd thank her for thinking of my future. I'd thank her for loving me and taking care of me the only way she knew how." I bite my lip as I look up. Adam's eyes are completely focused, urging me on. "I'd tell her that I miss her so much."

He pulls me toward him as I sob into his shoulder. "You're going to be okay," he says, planting a kiss on my forehead. "Because you have a bigger heart than anyone I've ever met. And my mom always says that life is a game and he, or she, who has the biggest heart wins."

I pull back to look him in the eye. "Thank you for everything. For bringing me here, for making me laugh, for knowing exactly what to say. Thank you for loving me."

He smiles as he shakes his head. "You're going to be thanking me for that for a very long time 'cause you're never getting rid of me."

CHAPTER EIGHTEEN

Relentless Storm

BY THE TIME we walk out of the hotel, the rain is pouring onto the streets of downtown Raleigh. We had planned to walk the half-mile to the restaurant, but that's not going to happen now. Adam finds a place to park in the parking deck on Blount Street and we race through the rain to meet Senia and Eddie. We pass a crowd of people standing outside The Pour House Music Hall waiting to be let in for the next show.

"I hope you don't mind, but I invited a couple of my buddies from Duke," Adam says as he opens the door for me at Bida Manda. "They're a year younger than me so don't hesitate to punch them if they come on to you."

"Isn't that *your* job?" I say as we approach the hostess.

"I'm on probation, remember?"

I sigh as I pull my wet hair into a low ponytail. "Why

do I always go for the bad boys?"

The hostess leads us to a table and I immediately spot Senia waving at me from the back of the room where they sit at the end of a very long table. She bolts out of her chair and we run to each other as if we haven't seen each other in four years instead of just four weeks. We hug and I yelp as she lifts me off the floor.

"Happy birthday!" she shouts.

"Save some of that energy for later, sexy," I say, and she growls as she puts me down.

"You're just so hard to resist in your wet T-shirt." She hooks her arm in mine and waves at Adam as she drags me to the table.

Adam's two friends are there and so is Eddie. Adam and his friends do a secret handshake before he sits on the end of the table next to his buddies and I sit across from him next to Senia.

"Claire, this is Rolly and Ian," he says, pointing a thumb at Ian next to him.

Rolly is a big guy, possibly taller than Adam and built like a linebacker. Ian is almost as hot as Adam, with his perfectly symmetrical facial features and icy-blue eyes, though he's a bit scrawnier. By the time dinner arrives, I've learned that Rolly and Ian are stepbrothers who also happen to be best friends. Their parents got married ten years ago and now they share a dorm at Duke. Their dorm was next to Adam's two years ago and they met when Adam punched a hole through their wall.

Rolly's chubby cheeks plump up as he grins at me. "But he went to anger management so he's all better now."

"She already knows about that," Adam groans as he reaches for his glass of water and pushes it across the table toward me.

This is our routine every time we go out to eat so it's second nature to him now. I finish the last two gulps in my almost empty glass and accept his glass.

"Yeah, but does she know about the time you threw Mike's laptop out the window?" Ian asks, his eyebrows perking up.

"Let's not go into all the shit the Incredible Adam broke in his fits of rage." Adam shakes his head in a can-you-believe-these-guys expression.

I smile, but I'm silently wondering how he managed to change from being such a tyrant into the person he is now. We've been so busy trying to fix me; we haven't delved enough into his pain.

The rest of the dinner is fun, and I actually have my first sip of alcohol when we all toast to my birthday. The waitress is in a good mood, so she allows me to use my expired ID when Eddie orders us each a champagne cocktail, which is just champagne with a flavored sugar cube.

"To the birthday girl," Eddie says, raising his glass and we all follow suit.

Adam turns to me. "To the birthday girl. The girl who stole my heart and my water."

My first sip of alcohol isn't so bad, but Adam insists I'm not allowed to drink more than one glass. Within two sips, I'm already feeling warm and frisky. I smile at Adam across the table as my foot grazes his shin. His left eyebrow shoots up and I wink at him. He reaches for my drink and slides it across the table so it's next to his empty bowl.

"I think you should stick to water." I slide my foot farther up his leg and he grabs it under the table. "Look at the time. We'd better get going before we miss the show."

After we settle the check, Ian and Rolly head home and we head next door. The crowd outside The Pour House is thinning as people hustle inside to get the best view of the stage at this intimate music hall. The outside of The Pour House looks like any dive bar. The inside is dark and crowded with some pool tables and standing room only in front of the stage. I've been here once before to watch a local indie band called Death Puppy, which turned out to be three nerdy hipsters performing an acoustic set of their mostly electronic music.

"Who's playing tonight?" I ask as a pushy crowd herds us toward the bar.

"Chris Knight. It's a secret performance for his local fans."

Senia and I look at each other and she immediately throws her arm around my shoulder to pull me aside. Eddie and Adam look on from a few yards away in confusion as she presses me up against a wall and gets in my face.

"You can't freak out, Claire, or he's going to know. He's going to know that Chris is your ex and it will all be downhill from there. No guy wants to find out their girlfriend used to be with a fucking rock star. Don't freak out."

My heart pounds against my chest, probably dying to get away from the oncoming musical assault. I can barely listen to his songs when they come on the radio or MTV. There is no way I'll make it through an entire concert of his music while standing just a few feet away from him.

"Are you seriously implying I need to endure the next three hours of torture? No! I want out of here. What if he sees me?"

"Claire?"

The sound of Joanie Tipton's lazy drawl makes my skin prickle.

"Claire, is that you?"

I turn to my right and Joanie is with Christa Monk and Veronica Evers. I don't know if Joanie has shared my secret with her two best friends, but the bored looks on their faces tells me she probably hasn't. My mind flashes quickly to two days after Joanie saw me in the hospital—the day I finally worked up the nerve and energy to go to Joanie's dorm and beg her not to tell anybody. The truth was, I really didn't care what Joanie or any of her cronies thought about me. I just didn't want it to get back to Chris.

"Joanie," I say, trying to keep my voice level.

"You're here to see Chris? Are you two back together?"

Christa and Veronica's eyes widen at this revelation.

"No, we're not. I was actually just leaving."

Senia grabs my arm. "No, we're not. We're just getting some drinks. Today's Claire's twenty-first birthday."

She casts Joanie a deadly look, daring her to fuck up my birthday. Joanie sighs, already bored with us, when Adam appears at my side.

"Are you okay, babe?" he asks, and Joanie's eyes light up at the sight of him.

"I'm fine."

I can't leave now. Joanie is bound to run onto the stage and scream my secrets into the microphone if we're not here to stop her. And she'd love to point out to Chris that I'm here with someone else—not that he'd care. I'm sure he's moved on—many times.

"I think I need a drink," I say, looking up at Adam.

He scrunches his eyebrows together. "Are you sure?"

I nod. It's about the only thing I'm sure of right now.

"Enjoy the show, Joanie," I say as I push Adam toward the bar.

I don't want to introduce him to Joanie. The last thing I need is for her to pretend she's drunk so she can accidentally spill some secrets like she did at Senia's twentieth birthday party—before I knew Joanie was only pretending to be my friend so she could get close to Chris.

Adam orders us both a beer then glares at me as he leans up against the bar. "Something's wrong."

The impulsive side of my brain is screaming at me to just tell him. This night is going to suck whether I tell him or not. The rational side of my brain is begging me to keep my mouth shut. I finally have someone who makes me feel happy; someone who might understand the mistakes I've made if I tell him in a more neutral environment. This is definitely not the place to come clean.

"I'm fine. I'm just really excited." I take a swig of the beer, which is bitter and kind of gross compared to the sweet champagne.

The sound crew finishes setting up the instruments on stage and I can feel the anticipation building in the crowd.

"Let's go see if we can squeeze in closer to the stage," he says, grabbing my hand.

"No!" Senia and I shout in unison.

Adam and Eddie glare at us.

"We should stay next to the bar in case Claire wants to get shitfaced for her birthday," Senia says.

"Yeah, I may want to get shitfaced."

Adam shakes his head. "You are *not* getting drunk tonight."

"It's my birthday and I'm twenty-one. I think that's my decision, buddy."

He frowns at me. He knows something is up. I'm not acting like myself. I set the glass of beer on the counter and flag the bartender down to ask him for some water.

Adam leans close to me, puts his lips next to my ear, and whispers, "Do you want to tell me what the fuck is going on?"

The bartender looks at me and I shout, "A glass of water, please!"

The bartender looks annoyed at my request, but he quickly fills a glass with some ice and water and slides it across to me. I take a long swig, letting the icy liquid cool the spicy food, and the secrets, burning inside me. I don't feel well.

I turn to Adam and his nose bumps mine. I can feel the heat of his breath on my mouth and I want to kiss him—not just to make him forget about the question he just asked. I want to kiss him to burn the memory of his lips into my brain because I have a bad feeling everything is going to change after tonight.

"Can we talk about it after the show?" I ask, and my stomach clenches as I realize this is not a stall tactic. I'm ready to tell him. I *will* tell him everything.

He nods then plants a soft kiss on my lips. I set my glass of water down on the bar and throw my arms around his neck. I need to feel his warmth. He wraps his arms around my waist and chuckles in my ear.

The crowd behind me explodes with cheers and

applause and I know what I'm going to see if I let go of Adam and turn around. I tighten my grip on his neck as my heart pounds against his.

"Claire, the show's starting," he says, his voice strained from how tightly I'm holding onto him.

I finally release my grip and he smiles down at me as he nods toward the stage. I close my eyes as I turn around.

You can do this. Just open your eyes and get it over with.

I slowly open my eyes and there he is.

CHAPTER NINETEEN

Relentless Music

THE BLUE SPOTLIGHTS cast a melancholy glow over the stage as Chris positions himself on his stool in front of the microphone. The drummer behind him is ready to go. It's Jake. I turn to the guy holding the bass guitar on Chris's right and I see Tristan. Jake and Tristan are Chris's old band mates who he basically dumped to go solo last year. It seems they were able to set aside the colossal grudge they've been carrying to play this gig.

Chris finally looks up from his guitar and my heart flutters. He looks exactly the same as he did a year ago. The same messy brown hair; the same dark eyes that turn down slightly at the corners, giving him that lost puppy dog look; the same full lips I've kissed a million times. I can't see if he still has the nose piercing, but I can see the light glinting off a new lip piercing. He's even wearing a ratty black UNC hoodie he wore when we were together. I don't know why I expected him to look different. I've been carefully avoiding his music videos and magazine articles, though I did read the *Rolling Stone* article only because it was in the employee restroom at the café for weeks and I was feeling a bit masochistic that day.

I glance around the room and everybody is so excited. You can feel the energy in the air shifting, as if everyone in this room is holding their breath waiting for those first few notes. The ticking sound of Jake's drumsticks tapping the rim of the drum focus my attention back on the stage.

Finally, Chris brings his lips to the microphone and speaks in that soothing voice with just a hint of a rasp. "What's up, Raleigh?"

The crowd cheers and some people shout back, "What's up, Chris?"

I feel as if I'm fifteen again and watching him play on the living-room floor for the first time when he played "In Your Eyes" by Peter Gabriel. Chris was always light-years ahead of his band mates—an old soul. He loved classic rock and blues. He made me listen to Miles Davis' greatest hits over and over until I could name each song just from hearing the first few notes. He was obsessed with music and that obsession made his dreams a reality.

A tear slides down my cheek as my heart swells with pride. I made the right decision breaking up with Chris. If he had stayed in Raleigh, none of this would have been possible.

The first notes of the song play and it's an up-tempo song about a girl who writes love notes. This song is not about me and, though I know it shouldn't matter, I really don't want to imagine it's about a real person.

Adam slips his arms around my waist and I smile as I lean my back into his chest. He kisses the top of my head as the song changes and I hear the first few notes of "Sleepyhead." I clench my teeth together and take a deep breath. If I can make it through this, I can make it through the rest of the night. Adam deserves it.

"You're shaking," Adam says in my ear, and I can barely hear him over the music.

"I'm fine!" I yell, but I don't turn my face toward him. I'm afraid he'll see what I'm feeling.

I do still miss Chris. This is why I never watch MTV or listen to the radio. It's why I deleted all his songs from my music collection and stashed everything that reminds me of him in boxes that are now collecting dust in Senia's parents' garage. I miss him. Every day.

I close my eyes and take another deep breath as he belts the chorus with so much emotion in his voice; it's no wonder all these girls are in love with him.

Adam leans down and presses his lips to my ear. "Remember the excuse you gave me when you rejected my offer to take you on a date?"

I think about the day he almost ran me over with his

truck when I was running away from the party, and Joanie, five weeks ago. I told him I couldn't go to lunch with him because I was sleeping in late.

It dawns on me that he's listening to "Sleepyhead" and thinking of that day.

I turn around and face him because I can't watch Chris and listen to this song *and* listen to Adam say this all at the same time. Adam lifts my chin and his eyes search my face for something. He knows something is off, but he can't quite figure it out. I force a smile, but he doesn't look convinced. I guzzle down the rest of my glass of water and finally the song ends. I let out a deep sigh as I turn around again.

The rest of the set is comprised of songs I don't think were inspired by me and a few covers. I'm feeling really good about myself for making it through the entire concert until the last song starts.

I've never heard the title track of Chris's album, *Relentless*. The single hasn't been released yet, but as soon as I hear the first few lines, I know it's about us.

"We kissed under the trees, and talked about missing things. I wish I could have held you in; held in the heat of your breath; held onto you and I at our best."

I do the one thing I think can save me from this moment. I spin around, pull Adam's face to mine, and kiss him. Not a hard, hungry kiss, but a slow, sensual kiss. The kind of kiss that makes time stop and everything disappear.

All I can feel is the curve of his mouth as it fits into mine. All I can smell is the faint hint of beer on his lips. All I can taste is the slightly sweet alcohol on his tongue.

"Having fun?" Joanie shouts.

"Ouch!" Adam yelps as I accidentally bite down on the tip of his tongue.

"Sorry!" I stroke his cheek and kiss the corner of his mouth, trying to ignore the fact that somewhere behind me Joanie is watching us.

"I'm okay," he says, then licks my cheek to prove it.

"Ew!" I squeal and he laughs.

"Aren't you two adorable?" Joanie yells into the back of my head.

She's obviously drunk. I should ignore her, but I'm so tired of her shit. I turn around and look her in the eye so she knows I know she's there. Then I turn back to Adam and kiss him—hard this time.

I can hear her cackling behind me and I break away before I round on her. "Fuck off, Joanie!"

"You sure moved on quickly. What would Chris think?"

I take a step forward to get in her face and Adam's hands lock around my arms. "Chris and I aren't together anymore!"

"You know what I'm talking about!"

The song ends and she smiles as she spins around, cups her hands over her mouth, and shouts, "*CHRIS!*

CLAIRE GAVE YOUR BABY UP FOR ADOPTION!"

The room is dead silent as Chris's eyes dart over the crowd toward Joanie's voice and lock on me. I'm frozen. This can't be happening.

Then Adam's hands fall away from my arms and I know I'm alone. I'm more alone in this moment than I have ever been in my life, with the weight of hundreds of eyes pressing in on me.

CHAPTER TWENTY

Relentless Decisions

BEFORE ANYBODY CAN stop me, I dart for the exit. I dodge Senia as she reaches for me, pushing aside anyone who gets in my way. I need to get out of here. I burst through the exit onto Blount Street and the rain pours down on me, giving new meaning to the name Pour House.

I glance up and down the street, trying to figure out which direction we came from the hotel, but I can't see anything I recognize through the relentless rain. It doesn't matter. I probably won't be staying at the hotel tonight anyway. Adam won't want anything to do with me after this.

I take off in the direction we came from the restaurant and race past Bida Manda. I've taken no more than ten steps before someone grabs my wrist and spins me around, but it's not who I expect.

It's Chris.

"Oh, God," I whimper.

It's happening. The day I've been dreading for almost a year.

"What the fuck?" he shouts, looking as confused as I felt the day I found out I was pregnant. "Claire, please tell me it's not true."

"I'm sorry," I whisper over and over. "I'm so sorry."

I'm only vaguely aware of the crowd forming around us. The hands are everywhere, reaching for me, reaching for him. Suddenly, we're both being pulled away. My feet leave the pavement and I'm floating toward an open car door. I'm stuffed inside and the door is slammed shut. The tires squeal as the car drives off.

I look to my right and Chris is leaning forward with his hands clutching his hair. "How could you do this to me?"

"I was scared and I didn't want to ruin your life."

"After everything we went through." He shakes his head, but he still won't look at me.

I don't know what's worse, knowing that Chris knows or knowing that Adam knows and I can't be there with him to explain.

"You need to take me back."

"They'll mob you."

"I don't care. My friends are there."

He finally sits up and glares at me. "I don't get it. We talked about having kids."

"When we were older. Not now. We weren't ready. You think if you'd had a choice you would have chosen to start a family and give up everything you've worked for?"

"I didn't *have* a choice!"

The anguish in his voice makes the hair on my arms stand up and the tears come faster than the rain. "I'm sorry I didn't tell you, but I'm not sorry that you got to live your dream." He watches the tears rolling down my face and I can feel him getting anxious. "I saw you tonight; all those girls screaming and crying for you. You can't tell me you'd give all that up to be stuck with me in some fucking suburb in Raleigh with a mortgage and a screaming baby? That's not what you wanted then and it's definitely not what you want now."

"You're crazy if you think I'd rather have this." He moves toward me and I don't flinch when he takes my face in his hands and brushes the tears from my cheeks. Not even a little. "You don't know me at all if you think I'd rather lose you *and* my child."

The palms of his hands are warm against my damp skin, but his fingers are calloused from strumming those steel guitar strings. Suddenly, I'm back in my bedroom at the Knight house where Chris left me over a year ago.

"You know we're both going to regret this," he says as he cradles my face in his hands.

"I know, but I don't care."

He kisses me and my entire body relaxes as I lie back on my bed. This is what Chris and I are meant for and I need it just one more time before it's over. I need to feel him moving inside me. I need to feel the weight of him on top of me. I need to feel safe with him one last time.

He lays his palms flat on either side of my head then runs his tongue over my top lip. A chill passes through me and pulses between my legs.

He pulls his head back and looks me in the eye. "I love you, Claire. I'll never stop loving you."

I grab the back of his neck and pull him to me. I wrap my legs around his waist and he grinds against me. There are too many layers of clothing between us. I reach for the button on his jeans and he moves my hand away as he kisses my neck.

"Slow down. We have all night."

His hand slides under my shirt as he gently sucks on my earlobe. I lift my back so he can undo my bra. I hastily peel off my tank top and bra then toss them aside. His fingers move lightly over my stomach until he reaches my breast. I draw in a sharp breath as his mouth covers my nipple. He licks me slowly and torturously, moving from one breast to the other as his hands unbutton my shorts. I lift my hips so he can pull them off, but he leaves my panties on. He takes his shirt and jeans off and tosses them onto the floor before he settles himself between my thighs again.

I can feel him stiff between my legs as his bare chest slides over my breasts. He kisses me and I gasp as his tongue parts my lips and thrusts inside my mouth. I clutch handfuls of his hair to keep his head *still. I don't want him to move. I don't want to ever stop kissing him.*

He grinds himself against me and my panties are soaked with the need to have him inside me. "Please, Chris," I whisper against his lips.

He kisses my neck as his lips travel down to the hollow of my throat. His tongue traces a line straight down my center until his face is between my thighs. He pulls my panties off and pauses for a moment. I look down to see what he's doing and he's staring at me.

"I'm going to miss this," he says, before he kisses me so lightly I can barely feel it.

His fingers part my flesh and he kisses me tenderly, teasing me with feather soft licks. The pleasure builds inside me and I grip the blanket underneath me to keep from writhing.

"Oh, Chris," I moan.

His tongue flicks and torments me into a frenzy and soon I find my release as my body convulses with ecstasy. He lays a soft trail of kisses over my belly and kisses each of my breasts before his mouth is on mine again. He kisses me tenderly and I can feel tears coming as I think of how much I'm going to miss him when he's gone.

He pulls his head back and looks down. His boxer briefs are gone and we both watch as he enters me slowly, my mouth opening wide in a silent gasp. I wrap my legs around his waist, beckoning him farther inside.

He takes his time, sinking in and out of me with the ease of a boat bobbing on a calm sea. That's what I am right now. I am a calm sea because the storm hasn't arrived yet. I know everything will be different when Chris leaves, but right now I want to enjoy this small sliver of peace.

He kisses the tears as they slide down my temples. I tighten my arms around his shoulders and crush my lips against his as he comes inside me.

He's kissing me and I can feel his new lip-piercing rubbing against my upper lip.

I push him hard in the chest and he falls back into his seat. "What are you doing?" I shriek.

Chris looks confused and I feel horrible. "Claire, I miss us. I still think about you every day."

"Don't do this."

"And you know what I think about? I think about how I can have any girl I want, except for you. How fucked up is that? Why are you doing this to me?"

"Everything's always about *you*. You left to pursue *your* dreams and, yes, I encouraged you to do it—heck, I *wanted* you to do it and I'm proud of you—but you never stopped to consider what you were leaving behind. You never thought of what it would do to me to lose my best friend and the one person who made me feel safe. You didn't take me into your home five years ago, Chris; *you* were my home. When I lost you, I lost everything."

He looks at me and I can feel the regret pulsing in waves off both of us, like two magnets repelling each other. "I'm going to get you back if it kills me."

I shift uncomfortably in my seat because I know this

isn't an empty promise. Chris gets what he wants. Always.

"Can you ask the driver to take me to 500 Fayetteville."

The car pulls up in front of the hotel entrance a few minutes later and the months of regret and agony we've both suffered is heavy between us. I wish I could reach across and tell him we're going to be together forever, like I once believed, but so much has changed.

With every choice you risk the life you would have had. With every decision you lose it.

I think of this quote every time I get the urge to tell anyone my secret. It's what I thought of when I decided not to tell Chris about the baby. Now it's time to decide again.

"It's over, Chris. And I'm sorry. I've never been more sorry in my life than I am for what I did to you. I will never stop being sorry. I will never lose this regret, but I do think I made the right decision. No matter how much it hurts. No matter how much it kills me to even admit that. I did what was right for both of us because now you have your dream career and I have someone who I love more than I thought I could ever love someone after you left. And, if you'll excuse me, I have to go to him." I kiss him on the cheek and he leans into me, wanting more. "I will love you for ever and ever, but I can't be with you. Goodbye, Chris."

CHAPTER TWENTY-ONE

Relentless Heartache

THE TRIP IN the elevator up to the sixth floor is excruciatingly slow and fast. I hope Adam is here. When I check my phone, I have eight texts and two voicemails from Senia, but nothing from Adam. I text Senia to let her know I'm okay and I'll call her later. I don't have the energy or the time to talk to her about this right now. I need to find Adam.

I knock on the door for room 608. Adam has the room key. He offered me the second cardkey, but I left it on the nightstand in the room thinking I wouldn't need it. If he doesn't answer, I'll just sit here and meditate for a while then call Senia to pick me up.

The door opens and Adam doesn't look at me as he steps back for me to come inside. He doesn't leave me much room and my chest brushes against his arm as I

207

slither past him. He closes the door and I take a few steps before I turn around. When he finally looks me in the eye, he doesn't speak. He's waiting for my explanation, which, by the looks of it, probably won't satisfy him.

"There are so many things I've done in my life that I regret, but right now there are two things that top that list. Number two is not telling you sooner. Number one is telling the hospital staff that I didn't want to know the sex of the baby."

I sink down onto the edge of the bed and force myself to remember that day. "Every time I get a fluttering in my stomach, I think of all the times my baby moved inside me. Every time I see a baby in public, I wonder." The mattress creaks as he sits next to me and the uneven distribution of our weight pulls me closer to him. "I don't know if you can understand what it's like to dream about a child with no face. To feel like a part of your heart will always exist just out of your reach."

He wraps his arm around my shoulder and pulls my face into his chest. "I'm sorry you had to go through that."

I wrap my arms tightly around his waist and as I think of all the nights I've lied awake agonizing over whether I should tell him my secret. He kisses my forehead as he takes my face in his hands and tilts my chin up.

"I love you so fucking much; it hurts to know that you've been carrying this inside of you." He pauses for a moment as he looks into my eyes and I can feel something bad is coming next. "It kills me to know that you didn't trust me enough to share it with me. And it scares me that you didn't share something so important with someone who was supposed to be your first love." He leans his forehead against mine and sucks in a sharp breath. "I love you, but I need some time to figure this out."

I pull my head back and nod because I couldn't speak if I tried.

"This doesn't mean I want to break up."

"I know," I whisper as I stand up and reach into my back pocket for my phone.

"Where are you going?"

"I have to call Senia to pick me up."

"You don't have to leave."

"I know, but you need some time to think and you'll probably want to do that without me here."

Just saying these words aloud makes my chest ache.

He stands and takes the phone from my hand. "Don't go. We need to talk. I don't want you to go."

I draw in a long stuttered breath as he takes my hand in his and leads me to the bed. He lays my phone on the nightstand and we lie next to each other, just staring at the ceiling for a few minutes. I think of all the times I could have told him; all the times I *should* have told him. Then I think of whether I should tell him that Chris kissed me. Did I kiss him back? I can't remember.

It feels like an eternity goes by before I finally speak.

"One of the foster homes I stayed in for a few months had a pregnant German Shepherd. Her name was April. April gave birth to three gorgeous puppies while I was there and I remember the look on April's face when my foster mother took the puppies away to clean them up. It was a mixture of confusion and gratitude." I pause for a moment as I remember the day I gave birth. Senia covered my face with a sheet so I couldn't see the baby as they pulled it out of me, cleaned it up, and wheeled it away. "I think I could be a good mother, but part of me thinks that might not be possible because a small part of me was grateful when they took my baby away from me. I just kept thinking how grateful I was that my baby would never have to go through what I went through with my mother."

Adam slips his hand under my neck and beckons me into his nook. I rest my head on his shoulder and breathe the smell of him mixed with the scent of rain.

"I think you'll make a great mother someday." He brushes my hair out of my face and strokes my cheek as he continues. "I saw you with those kids at Shell Island last Saturday. They loved you. Especially Ethan. I was getting a little jealous of you and Ethan."

"Shut up."

"Claire, I meant it when I said you have a bigger heart than anyone I've ever met. It may have been your wicked dance moves that attracted me to you initially, but it was the way you care for Cora that hooked me. I found myself thinking of good deeds I could do to impress you." I chuckle and he continues. "I know. It's pretty pathetic, but that's when I realized you were making me into the person I want to be; someone better than who I was before I moved to Wrightsville."

"It's not pathetic, but it's exactly the opposite of how I felt about you."

"So you're saying I made you into a worse person than you were before I moved in?"

"Yes, and no." He pokes my side and I push his hand away as I compose myself. "You pushed me to do things that made me uncomfortable. I was sleeping, literally. I was meditating sometimes ten times a day just to push the memories out of my mind. You were right when you said I was self-medicating. I haven't meditated once today, and today might be the second most stressful day of my life. You've helped me in ways that you can't even imagine."

"I haven't smoked in over a week."

"You haven't? Why?"

"I told you I wouldn't smoke around you and you spent the night in my apartment four times this week. Plus, I just haven't really been craving it as much." He slips his arm and shoulder out from under my head and flips onto his side so he's facing me and I do the same. "I need to ask you a question."

He pauses as if he's asking for permission to proceed. I milk the moment as I let my gaze wander over his face, committing his features to memory.

"I think we've reached the point where there's nothing I can't share with you."

"Where did you go after you left the concert?"

I heave a deep sigh and force myself not to turn away from him. "Chris's bodyguards stuffed us into a car to get us away from his screaming fans. We drove around while Chris and I talked." His gaze penetrates me and I finally look down. "He kissed me."

He sits up so suddenly my stomach flips from the sudden movement. "He kissed *you*? You didn't kiss him back?" He's staring at the wall. He's not looking at me anymore and it's making me nervous. "Please just answer the question. Did you kiss him?"

"I don't know." I sit up as he springs off the bed. "I was thinking about something and suddenly he was kissing me and I pushed him off as soon as I realized what was happening. I swear. I don't think I kissed him back."

"Are you saying he forced himself on you?"

The way he says this through gritted teeth makes me even more frightened for Chris.

"No! He would never do that."

He rubs his temples as he paces at the foot of the bed.

"Adam, please sit down."

He shakes his head as his mouth drops open, but he doesn't speak.

"Please say something."

He lets out a puff of laughter. "I can't believe all this time I've been competing with fucking Chris Knight. And you've been letting me play his songs in the truck."

"You're not competing with anybody. Chris and I are over. There is nothing between us." I rise from the bed and step in front of him. He tries to turn away and I grab the front of his shirt. "Listen to me." His eyes are fixed on the space above my head, but I don't care. "I love you, Adam, and only you. I love the way you smell. I love your voice." I reach up and touch his face. "I love the way your scruff rubs me raw. I love your eyes. I love your lips." He finally looks down as I press my finger against his lips. "I love waking up next to you. I love falling asleep in your bed. I love feeling you inside me. I love your stupid jokes. I love you more than I can ever fully express with words."

He kisses my fingertip and I breathe a sigh of relief as I realize I have just diffused a bomb. He squats down and wraps his arms around my thighs then picks me up. He rests his chin between my breasts as he looks up at me.

"I wish I had known earlier. If I'd known Chris Knight was your ex, I would've stepped up my game."

He leans his head back and I kiss him. Somehow, it feels like our first real kiss. It's the first kiss with no secrets between us.

I pull away to catch my breath and whisper. "Chris Knight has nothing on Adam Parker."

He tosses me onto the bed. I giggle as he pulls his shirt

off and crawls on top of me. "I'm going to wipe your memory clean of him."

He kisses me hard and our hands are everywhere as we undress each other.

"Sit up against the headboard," I order him, and he cocks an eyebrow. "Please."

He sits back and I straddle his lap as he slips a condom on. I rise up a little to get him underneath me and slowly ease myself down onto him. I dig my fingernails into his shoulders as a jolt of delicious pain sparks inside me.

I cradle his face in my hands and kiss him tenderly. His hands slide over my waist and lower back before he grips my butt. I tug his bottom lip with my teeth and he moans as we rock against each other in a slow, rhythmic motion.

He brings his hand forward and slides a finger between my folds. I gasp and throw my head back as he caresses my clit while thrusting himself deep inside me.

"Oh, Adam."

I arch my back and he takes my nipple into his mouth. His tongue teases my nipple as his finger strokes me. My thighs grow weak as I push myself up and down on him. I pull his face to mine and shove my tongue into his mouth as I grind myself against his fingers. He thrusts himself deeper inside me, hitting my core and crushing his hand between us. I pull his hand away and grind myself against his pelvis as I ride him, feeling the power trembling through our bodies as we clutch tightly to each other and climax together.

I rest my forehead against the top of his head as he kisses my shoulder. He moves onto my collarbone then kisses his way up to my mouth. We kiss like this for a long time, with him inside me, until I finally pull back.

I look him in the eye and ask the one question I've been afraid of knowing the answer to since we met. "Now that you know everything, can you still trust me?"

His chest is still heaving as he thinks about his answer and I lay my hand over his chest to feel his heartbeat. He grabs my hand and plants a soft kiss on my palm before he lays it back over his heart.

"I think I trusted you too easily," he says, and my stomach clenches as I prepare myself for what he's about to say. "But I wouldn't give my heart to someone I didn't trust. And you have my whole heart, Claire, so please be gentle with it."

I kiss his forehead and look him in the eye. "I'll be gentle. I wouldn't want to crush my favorite olive."

CHAPTER TWENTY-TWO

Relentless Love

IT TOOK SIX days to pack up all my stuff, put it in storage, and convince the admissions counselor at UNC to take me back as a sophomore. Okay, it took five days to convince the admissions counselor and one day to pack, but I got it done with the help of the most amazing boyfriend a girl could ask for.

"Knock, knock," Adam says as he writes *KITCHEN* on the box I just finished packing.

"Who's there?" I say, snatching the marker from his hand and writing *FRAGILE* on the same box.

"Leopard."

"Leopard, who?"

"Leopard with spots."

I glare at him from across the box we're both squatting next to. "You're kidding? This is what you're resorting to now?"

"Just making sure you're paying attention. Here's a good one." He takes the marker from my hand and places it on the kitchen counter as he stands. "I'm going to start competing again."

I stand up so I can look him in the eye. "Are you being serious now?" He nods and I pause for a moment before I throw my arms around his neck. "This is great! I'm so proud of you."

He laughs as he wraps his arms around my waist and lifts me onto the counter. "It's not a big deal. It's a small competition that takes place down in Florida at the end of this month. I'll be gone for a couple of days so I won't be able to see you that weekend."

I try not to let the disappointment show on my face. Now that I'm going back to school, weekends are the only time I'll be seeing Adam. He promised to drive from Wilmington to UNC every weekend—a two-and-a-half-hour drive. I know there will be times when both of us will have other plans or commitments and there may be times when we'll go weeks without seeing each other, but it will be worth it. It will all be worth it when I have my degree and I'm given the chance to mend a child's broken heart the way I wish someone had tried to fix mine.

"I wish I could be there to watch."

"You can," he says. "I can pick you up Friday night and we'll be in Florida at least six hours before the first heat."

"Yeah, with no sleep. I can't let you go into your first competition with no rest."

"What time does your last class end on Friday?"

"One."

"See. We can make it to Florida by ten. I'll get plenty of rest, assuming you can keep your hands off me."

He wiggles his eyebrows and I shake my head.

"Adam, you don't have to do this just to make me feel better about us being apart. I know there are going to be times when our schedules don't mesh. I'm a big girl. I can handle it."

He sighs as he leans his head back. "I just don't want us to get used to being apart."

I hook my legs around his waist and pull him closer. "We're going to be okay. We're going to spend the whole week of Thanksgiving together and four weeks during Christmas and New Year's. We're going to get sick of each other."

He doesn't look convinced. He looks the way I feel.

"You're assuming that I won't have to go to Hawaii for work."

I take a deep breath as I try to resist the urge to go into the bedroom and meditate. "We'll cross that bridge when we come to it."

"Ew! Are you guys having sex on the counter?" Senia squeals as she enters the apartment carrying a six-pack of beer and a six-pack of bottled water. "Well, don't let me stop you. Merry Christmas," she says, handing Adam the beer and me the water.

I slide off the counter and put the water down so I can give her a hug. "What did your dad say when you asked him for the day off?" I ask, cracking open a bottle of water and taking a long swig.

"He said if I took the day off he was going to fire me. That's only the third time this week he's used that one."

"You're such a spoiled brat," I say, shaking my head as I reach for another bottle of water.

"Yes, I am, which is why my dad is not firing me. He's buying me a new car."

"Shut up!"

Adam rolls his eyes as he scoots past us. "I'm going to check on Cora."

He scampers out of the apartment and leaves the door open on his way out. The storm that came the day of the concert has passed, leaving behind clear skies and a warm breeze that carries in the briny scent of the ocean.

Senia grabs a bottle of water and leans up against the counter. "Yep! My dad's getting me a new car and I'm giving you the Focus."

"I'm not taking your car."

I grab the marker off the counter and march into the living room to label some more boxes. She follows me and sits on top of the first box I kneel in front of.

"You *are* taking my car or I'm pushing it over a cliff. You need it, Claire. Adam can't always be the one making the effort to see you. A good relationship is a balance of give and take."

"I can't believe you want to give me your car just so I can see my boyfriend on the weekends."

"Well, I didn't say that was the only reason. The position of Senia's designated driver still hasn't been filled." I push her off the box and she falls onto the floor, spilling water over the front of her halter-top. "Hey!" she squeals as she flings a splash of water in my direction.

The water hits me in the face and I suck in a sharp breath before I compose myself and run for the kitchen to get a retaliatory bottle of water. That's when I see him standing just outside the front door.

Chris is wearing a Black Keys T-shirt and a gray beanie similar to the one he wore the day we met. His expression is serious as he stands with his hands behind his back and nods at me as if he can't say the word *hello* aloud. I look to Senia and she's dumbstruck as she gawks at him from where she sits on the floor. She's met him plenty of times, but not since he became famous.

Chris turns to her and waves. "Hey, Senia."

"Hhh-hey, Chris," she replies.

He smiles awkwardly and turns back to me. "Claire." The way he says my name makes my whole body ache. "Can we talk?"

We can't talk here, with Adam across the hall.

"How did you find me?"

He doesn't have to answer. He's got money coming out of every orifice now. That was a stupid question.

"I have something I want to show you." He pulls a large manila envelope out from behind his back.

A million possibilities race through my mind at once, but only one seems likely. "Follow me," I say as I walk to the bedroom without looking at Senia.

I don't want to know if she thinks inviting Chris into my bedroom is a bad idea. I need to know what's in this envelope because I know Chris wouldn't come all the way out here if it weren't important.

I close the door behind us as we enter my bedroom. The beds were here when I moved in so they're staying behind when I move out. The mattresses look so bare without the sheets and blankets. I sit down and he hands me the envelope as he sits next to me.

I look at him for a moment in the daylight and try to determine what's different about him. "You got rid of the nose ring?"

"Yeah, I took it out of my nose and popped it straight into my lip."

"That's gross."

"You're the one who had it in your mouth when you were kissing me."

"You kissed *me*!"

"Is that the official story you told your boyfriend?"

"It's the truth and his name is Adam."

"Your face is wet," he says as he reaches up and brushes a drop of water from my jaw.

The familiarity with which he touches me, the comfort and ease of reaching for someone who you once knew better than yourself, all of this is embedded in this single touch. The second his skin touches mine, a shudder travels through me.

I quickly push his hand away. "Don't do that," I whisper as I stare at the tattoos on his arms to keep myself from looking into his eyes.

Most of them I recognize, but there's a new one on the inside of his right forearm that wasn't there last year. I can only see half of it from this angle, but it's definitely a shattered heart. I begin unfolding the metal clasps on the envelope and he puts his hand over mine to stop me.

"Wait. I need to explain first." I push his hand away again and he leans forward, resting his elbows on his thighs. "I felt really lost after you left on Friday. I've been feeling lost for a long time. I come home to visit every once in a while and you're not there and my mom is a fucking saint, but—"

"Chris, I'm sorry I didn't visit Jackie on Saturday."

"No, don't apologize for that. I told her what happened and she understands."

"You told her?"

"Well, I told her I ran into you at the show, but I didn't tell her what you told me."

"Oh, thank God."

"And I didn't tell her you ripped my heart out."

He sits up and looks me in the eye and I feel like I'm sixteen again, waiting for him to tell me he loves me. His skin is so perfectly smooth. I stare at the bow of his lips the way I used to right before we were about to kiss. I wrench my eyes away to meet his gaze and his dark eyes glint with a hint of a smile that barely curls his lips.

"Claire, you don't have to keep hiding this. I'm going to fix it. I swear."

"You can't. This isn't something that can be fixed the way you fixed me."

"I'm not stupid. I know I can't get back what's not mine."

I don't know if he's talking about the baby or me, but I suddenly feel the need to meditate. I scoot back on the mattress and lay the envelope on my lap as I curl my legs underneath me.

"Then why are you here?"

"I'm here to tell you that I want to try. I talked to my lawyer about everything and he recommended a good adoption lawyer."

My heart pounds wildly as I anticipate the direction this conversation is going. I think I know what he's going to say, but what scares me the most is that I might not want to hear it.

"I've been talking to the lawyer this week and she's been talking to the agency that handled the adoption," he continues. "The guy at the agency thinks the couple who adopted our baby might still agree to an open adoption, since the baby's only four months old." I can't move or speak so he takes the envelope from me and pulls out a stack of papers held together with a paperclip. He sets the papers facedown on the bed and smiles. "Her name is Abigail. She lives in Raleigh."

"She?" I whisper as I press my lips together.

"Yeah, and she looks just like you."

He turns the stack of papers over and there's a picture clipped to the front. She's lying in a crib on top of a fuzzy cream-colored blanket. She's lying peacefully asleep and is almost bald, but I can still glimpse a tuft of soft blonde hair growing on the top of her head. Her top lip is much bigger than her bottom lip as her mouth hangs open in a silent O. She's clutching a piece of the blanket in her chubby fist the way I do when I sleep.

"Abigail," I whisper as I shake my head.

I still can't believe it. I've been calling her Baby in my mind for four months. Every night I say a prayer that Baby is safe and warm and loved. I can see from this picture alone that Abigail is all of those things and more.

"We might be able to see her soon, but I need to know that this is what you want."

I can't tear my eyes away from the picture, as if staring at it long enough will cause some kind of cosmic epiphany and I'll suddenly know what to do and say. I made the tough decision of giving her up four months ago so that I wouldn't have make these kinds of difficult decisions until I was old enough to know better.

She looks so peaceful. Will I ruin that just by being me?

Chris lifts my chin to tear my gaze away from the photo. "I can't do this without you."

The sound of Adam's voice in the apartment startles me. He's asking for me. I push Chris's hand away and stuff the papers back into the envelope just as Adam walks in.

"What's going on, Claire?" he asks, but his eyes are on Chris.

I shoot up from the bed with the envelope clutched in my hands. "He was just dropping off some documents. He's leaving now."

I push Adam back through the doorway, but his eyes are locked on Chris.

"I'm not leaving until you give me an answer," Chris says, and I can hear his voice behind me getting closer.

Adam resists me as I push him toward the living room. "Stop pushing me. I can control myself. I'm not a fucking child."

"Yes or no, Claire?" Chris asks.

I look over my shoulder at him and shake my head. "I

don't know."

"What is he talking about?" Adam asks.

I want to tell him. If I've learned anything over the past month it's that keeping secrets from the one you love is a recipe for disaster. But I don't want him to judge me if the answer is no. And I don't want to scare him away if the answer is yes.

"I'll tell you later," I say, and he glares at me incredulously.

"Are you fucking kidding me? After everything that just happened, you're going to give me that shit again?"

"Don't talk to her like that," Chris says, and I can hear the threat in his tone.

"Stay out of it, Chris," I warn him.

"You let him talk to you like that?"

"I said stay out of it!"

Adam pushes my hands off his chest. "Keep your secrets. I'm out of here," he says, and he storms out of the apartment.

Senia, who's been standing quietly in the kitchen this whole time, creeps toward the front door. "I have to get something from my car," she whispers.

"You deserve better than that, Claire," Chris says as he moves toward me. "You deserve someone who knows you and respects you."

"Adam respects me. You don't know him."

"Do *you* know him? How long have you two been

together?"

"It's none of your business," I say as he stops a couple of feet away from me.

"It *is* my business if you're planning to stay with him. I don't want someone like that around our daughter if they grant us visitation."

"He's not a monster. He has a right to question why you're here in my apartment after what happened last week."

He takes another step forward and I take a step back, bumping the backs of my legs against a box. "I don't want to talk about him," he says, taking another step forward so our faces are inches apart. "I came here for you and believe me when I say that I won't stop until I get you back." His fingers graze the side of my face and I hold my ground, unwilling to crumble for him. "Think about this. Think about what it will be like to hold her in your arms."

He kisses my forehead and leaves me with a handful of legal documents and a heart full of questions. I don't know if this is the best or the worst news Chris could have delivered to me, but a huge part of me has never felt more grateful for him. Chris has always known exactly what I need and he's always been willing to do whatever it takes to give it to me.

I take a deep breath and grab my keys off the breakfast bar. I lock the front door and head for the beach.

I find Adam sitting near the edge of the water and he

doesn't look at me as I sit next to him. I dig my hands into the warm sand and scoop up a handful. I let it fall slowly and watch as most of it is carried away on the breeze. I guess that's the way secrets are. They're only heavy when you're holding them. As soon as you let go, the significance of keeping those secrets hidden blows away and everything falls into place.

"My daughter's name is Abigail," I say, and he finally looks at me. "That's what he came to tell me. He thinks he can get his lawyer to arrange an open adoption."

"Is that what you want?"

I shrug as I wrap my arms around my knees. "I don't know if I could handle seeing her and leaving her. I've already done that once and it nearly destroyed me."

"But you wouldn't be leaving her forever this time."

We sit in silence for a long time until the sun begins to touch the horizon and Adam grabs my hand. "Come on. Let's see if the water has the answer."

He kisses my hand before he stands and pulls me up. "I love you, Claire. I'll support you whatever you choose to do. You know that, right?"

I smile as I breathe in this moment. "I do."

He pulls me toward the water and we trudge through the knee-high waves, in our clothes, until we're waist deep. A small wave crashes into me and I get a mouthful of ocean. He laughs as I spit out the salty water. Then he kisses me. The salt in my mouth mixes with the sweetness of his tongue and I can feel his smile curving against my mouth.

He pulls away as he looks into my eyes and doesn't say a word. He doesn't have to.

As soon as the sun begins to set, it seems to fall too quickly from the sky, like a heart in love. The relentless pull of love is a thousand times harder to fight than the tides. If you're lucky, you'll make it out before you drown. If you're even luckier, you're pulled under just long enough to wash away the sorrow. If you're really lucky, like me, you resurface just in time to find the one you love floating right beside you.

This story continues in *Pieces of You* (Book Two)
To find out how to purchase *Pieces of You*, go to:
http://cassialeo.com

"RELENTLESS"

We kissed under the trees
And talked about missing things
I wish I could've held you in
Held in the heat of your breath
Held onto you and I at our best

Memories chain me here
Holding my heart prisoner
Alone in this hotel room now
Can't stop dreaming of your kiss
Tomorrow I'll regret this

Your love is relentless
Holding me still
Relentlessly dreaming
Breaking my will
I wish you'd come with me
Leave it behind
Just pack up your things and
Say you'll be mine

You said you would miss us
Didn't know you could bluff
Are you moving on already?
Sleeping in someone else's bed
Fucking with someone else's head

I'm sinking, sinking
You've got my love and my time
I've got nothing, nothing
Relentless love and heartache are mine
You've got me, got me
But I can't make this call just to find
You don't want me

"SLEEPYHEAD"

Feels so wrong to want this
You look so broken there
A flicker in the mist
As tired as the air

Your head upon the pillow
It's time to bury bones
Outside a whispering willow
The limbs fall like stones

So frightened of the dark
You're my sleepyhead
Hiding with the stars
Put your dreams to bed
My sleepyhead.
You're my sleepyhead.

With eyes full of shadow
And a mouth full of glass
Gasps come so hollow
Your lips taste like ash

Don't waste your hours
Your time don't come cheap
Don't fall apart, baby
Just fall asleep

And I don't know why I can't kill this doubt
But I promise I'll put your pain to rest
If it means I never sleep again.

Relentless Playlist

"The A Team" by Ed Sheeran
"I Need Your Love" by Ellie Goulding feat. Calvin Harris
"All I Want" by Kodaline
"Omega" by Steve Aoki feat. Dan Sena and Missy Palmer
"Locked Out of Heaven" by Bruno Mars
"Waiting in Vain" by Bob Marley
"Thinking of You (Acoustic)" by Katy Perry
"Heart of Stone" by Iko
"Last of Days" by A Fine Frenzy
"Hometown Glory" by Adele
"If It Kills Me (Casa Nova Sessions)" by Jason Mraz
"Stubborn Love" by The Lumineers
"Wait" by M83

YouTube: http://bit.ly/relentlessplaylist

Spotify: http://bit.ly/relentlessplaylists

Turn the page for a preview of

Pieces of You

Shattered Hearts (Book Two)

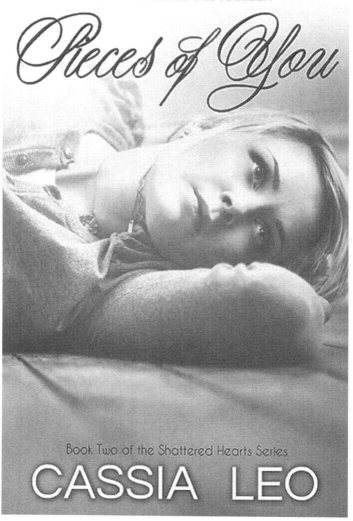

NEW YORK TIMES BESTSELLER

Pieces of You

Book Two of the Shattered Hearts Series

CASSIA LEO

Chapter One

CHRIS

THE SMELL OF sweaty bodies wafts toward the stage on a steamy puff of air as I pull out the last licks on "Relentless." The crowd goes wild. The girls in the front row, their eyes wild, clawing at the stage trying to reach my feet. I stare at them, mesmerized. All I can think is that Claire used to want me like that. At one time, Claire would have crawled across a desert for me.

Tristan shakes my arm to break my trance. I force a smile for the crowd. Take a bow and say my goodbyes to the good people of Charlotte, North Carolina.

We hop into Tristan's car after the show and head to Cary to christen his new house with some debauchery. I'm not in the mood to hang out tonight, but I'm also not in the mood to be alone. And I can't call Claire. It's almost midnight on a Thursday. She'll be asleep or studying.

And she has a boyfriend.

I chuckle out loud at this thought and Tristan looks at me as he drives down I-85. "What the fuck are you laughing at?"

"Nothing."

"You're cracking up, man. You need to get your head out of Claire's ass and have some fun tonight."

"What I need is to stop taking advice from you."

The past year without Claire is almost a blur. Just a mess of images, going from one show to the next, one hotel to the next, one drink to the next, one girl to the next. I don't remember much of it.

What I do remember is being utterly and completely miserable. It's just not fucking fair. I set off to Los Angeles to live the dream and I lose the love of my life, my dog dies, and now I've lost my daughter. Worst fucking year of my life. This isn't at all what I pictured when I decided to take that record deal.

When I let Claire convince me to take that record deal.

I never wanted to leave Claire. I knew it wouldn't end well. But I've always been a complete sucker for her. I've always done everything with the intent of making her happy.

For a year, I've replayed our last conversation a million times in my head.

"Stop calling me. Please."

"Claire."

"Stop saying my name. I have to go."

Then dead silence. For a whole year.

But I did just as she asked. I stopped calling. And I stopped saying her name. For a couple of months. Until I couldn't do it anymore and I called her, only to find her phone was disconnected and she wasn't talking to my mom anymore. Just like that. She was gone.

It made no sense to me then, but now I know why she did it. Fuck. As much as it hurts and pisses me off, I even understand it.

Tristan changes lanes to head for the 421 interchange, but I quickly protest.

"Stay on I-85. You'll get there faster."

He shakes his head because he knows I'm just torturing myself. If we stay on I-85 we'll have to drive through Chapel Hill. I'll see all the street names I haven't seen in more than a year. Places where Claire and I shared a million memories during her freshman year at UNC.

One thing I can say for Tristan, he's good at keeping quiet when it's necessary. Seventy silent minutes later, we pull into the curved driveway of Tristan's mini-mansion in Cary. Even with Tristan speeding down I-85, Jake and Rachel beat us here. Rachel drives like a crazy person.

"Well, look who woke up and decided to join us," Rachel remarks as I climb the steps to the front door. Her eyes are wide and her mouth hangs open, a bad zombie-like imitation of me at the end of the show tonight.

"Fuck off. Don't make me do my impression of Psycho Rachel."

She rolls her eyes at me as if she's not afraid, but this shuts her up. She doesn't want anyone to remember the crazy way she behaved last year when she and Jake broke up for a few months. It's difficult not to go a little crazy when you realize you've lost the one thing you're living for.

Thirty minutes later, the house is crawling with at least forty people, most of whom I've never seen in my life. Tristan and I switch roles for the night and I take his usual spot on the corner of the sofa, sipping a Miller Lite, while he serves drinks and chats up his audience from the breakfast bar in the kitchen. Every time I look up, I catch some girl I've never met staring at me. It's only a matter of time before one of them approaches me or tries to sit next to me and spark up a conversation.

As expected, a skinny blonde with a red bandana tied around her head as headband and cutoff jean shorts sits next to me. Her red lipstick has left a perfect half-moon mark on the martini glass she's clutching in her left hand. She smiles at me, but I don't return the smile. Instead, I look out across the living room and dining area to the kitchen where Tristan is pouring some vodka into a shot glass.

"Are you okay?" the girl asks in a voice that reminds me a little of my mom's. A soft, southern lilt that you can tell she's trying to hide.

I glance at her again and she's wearing a look of great concern that makes me a little sick to my stomach. "I'm fine. Thanks."

Tristan downs the shot he just poured and slams the shot glass down on the counter. I take a long swig of beer, as if this will help me keep up.

"You rocked the show tonight," the blonde continues. "I'm Charlie."

I nod, but I can't bring myself to say, Nice to meet you. It would just be too phony. And I really want this girl to get the hint. She's not hooking up with me tonight, or ever.

"Do you live here with Tristan?" she asks. "I'll bet you two have a lot of fun here. Even if it is pretty quiet."

I turn to look at her and she smiles now that she has my full attention. "Charlie?"

"Yes?"

"I'd really like it if you could leave me alone right now."

She narrows her eyes at me. "I was just trying to talk to you. You don't have to be a prick about it."

"I believe I was pretty polite. But I can be rude if you'd like."

She rolls her eyes as she stands up and heads for the breakfast bar. I almost breathe a sigh of relief before another girl heads in my direction, as if she was just waiting for Charlie to leave so she could pounce on me. I let out a sigh of exasperation instead.

"Was that your girlfriend?" asks the girl with the dark hair that falls in waves over her fake boobs.

"No, my girlfriend isn't here tonight," I reply.

She looks stricken. "Oh, you're with that Dakota girl, right?"

I grit my teeth at the mention of Dakota Simpson; the Disney star I fucked twice and almost had to get a restraining order to get her to stop calling me and showing up at my concerts.

"No, I'm not with her."

"Oh. I heard she's all coked-up anyway."

She's not, but I don't bother correcting her. I don't need to defend Dakota from untrue rumors. That's a sure way to perpetuate the rumors about us being together.

The girl with the boobs looks around awkwardly as she realizes she's getting nowhere with me. "Well, nice meeting you."

She shoots up from the sofa and heads toward the backyard patio where she came from. I feel a twinge of guilt for shooting down these girls, but I'm not interested in an easy fuck tonight.

I pull my phone out of my pocket and open up the picture I have set as my new background wallpaper. My heart aches just looking at it. I take another long pull on my beer, then I place the empty bottle on the coffee table.

Abigail is lying peacefully on a fluffy, cream-colored

blanket; an angel I never knew I had until three weeks ago. I clench my teeth to hold back the flood of emotions I'm feeling: the rage from being kept in the dark; the pain from losing everything important to me; and the fear that I may never get it back.

Fuck that. I'm getting Claire back if it's the last fucking thing I do.

———✒———

Want more?

To find out how to purchase *Pieces of You* go to:

http://cassialeo.com

Acknowledgements

I've been writing books for longer than I care to admit, but I've never had more people to thank than now. This book was my brainchild, but it was birthed through the labor of many selfless souls.

Special thanks go to my old and new beta readers: Kristin Shaw, Jordana Rodriguez, Michael Finn, Sarah Rabe, Carissa Andrews, Kim Box Person, and Sheri Zilinskas. Extra special thanks go to Sarah Rabe who fact-checked me on some important details about the foster care system. Your willingness to share your personal experience added so much depth to Claire's character and I am just so proud of the woman and friend you have become. Michael and Sheri: What can I say other than you two are what the crazy person who invented beta readers intended. There are no words to adequately describe how grateful I am for your feedback.

So much gratitude and awe go to the magnificent Sarah Hansen at Okay Creations. Your professionalism made this experience painless. Your talent made this cover relentlessly breathtaking.

An enormous thank you goes out to all the book bloggers and reviewers who offered their time and expertise to assist with this book release, especially Karen Anderson at Book Crush Book Reviews. You are all so friggin' amazing. Your support of indie authors, not just me, is awe-inspiring. I hope I wasn't too difficult to work with.

There are no words to express my gratitude to the many friends and family members who offered their support in so many ways during the writing of this book. You are all saints for putting up with my disappearing acts, the lack of home-cooked food, having to repeat your sentences two and three times, and my endless pleas for feedback.

And a huge thank you to all the readers who contacted me during the months I was writing *Relentless*. Your enthusiasm and kindness motivated me to get through one of the most hectic deadlines of my career. Your support has made my childhood dream of being a professional author a reality! I love you all so much and hope you all continue to get in touch with me often.

Want more?

To find out how to purchase *Pieces of You* go to:

http://cassialeo.com

Other books by Cassia Leo

CONTEMPORARY ROMANCE

Relentless **(Shattered Hearts #1)**

Pieces of You **(Shattered Hearts #2)**

Bring Me Home **(Shattered Hearts #3)**

Abandon **(Shattered Hearts #3.5)**

Black Box **(stand-alone novel)**

PARANORMAL ROMANCE

Parallel Spirits **(Carrier Spirits #1)**

EROTIC ROMANCE

Unmasked Series

KNOX Series

LUKE Series

CHASE Series

About the Author

New York Times and *USA Today* bestselling author Cassia Leo loves her coffee, chocolate, and margaritas with salt. When she's not writing, she spends way too much time watching old reruns of *Friends* and *Sex and the City*. When she's not watching reruns, she's usually enjoying the California sunshine or reading—sometimes both.

Made in the USA
Middletown, DE
30 April 2015